Ordination

T0303497

Scott A. Kaukonen

The Ohio State University Press
Columbus

Library of Congress Cataloging-in-Publication Data

Kaukonen, Scott A.
Ordination / Scott A. Kaukonen.
    p. cm.
    ISBN 0–8142–0991–2 (cloth : alk. paper)—ISBN 0–8142–9067–1
(cd-rom) 1. United States—Social life and customs—Fiction. I. Title.
    PS3611.A85073 2005
    813'.6—dc22
                        2004025022

Paper (ISBN: 978-0-8142-5731-9)

Cover design by Dan O'Dair
Type set in Granjon

Ordination

For my parents

Contents

Acknowledgments

I would like to thank the following people: Jack Ridl, who gave me an "F" on my first college paper and in the process opened the world to me; my friends and colleagues in Tucson and Columbia, especially those teachers and writers under whose watch these stories first took shape; the Association of Writers and Writing Programs for the Prague Fellowship; The Chicago Tribune Foundation for the Nelson Algren Award; *Third Coast* for being first; The Ohio State University Press for the opportunity to share these stories with others; my family, especially my siblings, Steve, Angee, and Brenda; Kirstin, who knows the sacrifices required; and finally, my parents, Rev. Aaron and Janet Kaukonen, whose unconditional love has made all this possible.

Ordination

I f my mother were to tell the story, she would begin in the basement nursery of the church.

A random assortment of brightly colored, barrel-shaped, Fisher-Price figures—a farmer, a bus driver, a policeman, a classroom full of children and a dog—are scattered across the stained blue carpet, disbursed and then abandoned by my 19-month-old self. In the corner, an empty mechanical baby rocker clicks back and forth, back and forth, and the boiler in the adjoining closet whistles and rattles like a bull about to charge. The windowless pea-green walls are stark and bare, and the room cold. She is exhausted from the six-hour ride through the gray Midwestern winter rain to the steady rnt . . . rnt . . . rnt of the windshield wipers, and her breasts are sore from feeding my three-month-old brother, who is screaming like an Old Testament prophet. Her knees press into the hard floor as she pulls a thin, blue blanket around his tiny shoulders, cradling him against her body and whispering, *shh . . . shh . . . shh*, in his ear. She knows she has a run in her nylons and that it's only getting worse and she knows she has an extra pair that she tucked into her purse before we left home. But she does not think of the nylons, does not think of the damp splotches on her blue dress where my brother has dribbled his milk, does not think about the button on her blouse that I have pulled loose in protest of her order to *settle down*. Instead, she thinks about sound, how it moves, how it carries, how it slides through walls and ceilings, and she hopes the cold air swallows the sound of my brother's screams, of her voice telling me to get *down from there*.

Upstairs, in a dark-paneled room just off the narrow, pew-filled auditorium, her husband—my father—sits at one end of a long folding table that has dried wads of bubble gum rimmed around the bottom edge. His hands are clasped before him atop the table, resting between a barely touched paper cup of black coffee and his black dog-eared leather-bound King James Bible. His notes for tomorrow's sermon—typed by my mother on the Smith-Corona that was his parents' wedding present—are tucked away somewhere near Nehemiah. The board of deacons—men in ill-fitting suits and wide ties, men with receding hairlines and a tooth-and-nail grasp of the Bible, men who are farmers and factory workers with callused hands and grease-stained fingernails, men who've never been to college, but who have been to war—fill the remaining metal folding chairs around the table.

If my mother could, she would bow her head and say another prayer for my father, a prayer for strength and courage and peace and the right answers that will earn him this job, his first real job, his first pulpit as the pastor of the First Baptist Church of Paradise, Michigan. She would pray this if she could, if she had a moment, but my little brother just keeps crying that high-pitched, ear-piercing scream, never quite emptying those lungs, and now I'm climbing the side of the crib—since when did he learn to do this, she thinks—and she fears that I'm going to fall, crack my head open, have to be taken to the hospital for stitches—how would I explain it—so from her knees she's trying to hold my brother close to her sore chest with one arm and pull me off the crib with the other.

And that's when the elderly woman—Mrs. Brubaker, my mother will soon learn, a woman who will torment my mother for years with her harsh judgments and sharp tongue before growing gracious in the final stages of ovarian cancer—appears in the doorway. She wears a floral dress that announces itself with all the fervor of a Pentecostal evangelist, filled with purples and yellows and oranges and reds—Mother can't sort all the colors out right now; it will take several potluck dinners. The woman has long white gloves, a wide-brimmed white hat and a plastic white purse with metallic gold clasps, dangling from the crook of a pasty, flabby-skinned arm. No one has told her that she shouldn't wear white shoes between Labor Day and Memorial Day, but my mother senses she isn't a woman who listens to the opinions of others.

"I wouldn't let him climb on that if I were you," the woman says. "He could fall."

My mother nods, it's all she can do, she's whispering to me, urgently, to get down, now, trying to be authoritative without granting my actions more significance than they contain—just a toddler testing his new found motor skills. My brother presses upward into the stratospheric reaches of auditory perception, impossibly so it seems for such tiny lungs.

The woman moves forward into the nursery, purposefully, even dog-matically, passes my mother and makes her way to the lone chair in the room—an old wooden rocker that my mother has been trying to use to calm my brother. The woman removes the strap of the plaid diaper bag from the armrest, places it on the floor and claims the seat as hers. She crosses one doughy leg—dark stocking rising up her thick calf—over the other and begins to rock gently, looking upwards toward the water-stained ceiling.

There are no introductions, no exchanges of pleasantries. The woman doesn't bother to offer my mother any assistance with the chil-dren, doesn't inquire as to our ages or to the discomfort of the drive. She says nothing of herself, does not reveal that her husband is the elder statesman on the board of deacons. My mother will eventually learn that both Mrs. Brubaker and her husband have been life-long members of the church, and that their fathers were charter members at the turn of the century when services were held in a barn. But the woman does not say this now. There will be time for such exchanges later.

"Your husband seems so young," she says. Her white hair is piled high in a beehive that makes my mother think momentarily of the Andrews Sisters.

"Twenty-six," my mother replies. In her frustration with me, she overcompensates with her voice and sounds artificially cheerful—like the bad actress my father will one day tell her she is.

"Handsome though," the woman says. "And bright."

My mother forces a smile, clutches my brother close to her chest with both hands and awkwardly rises to her feet. My brother's tiny fingers grip the edge of her blouse, tug it downward, revealing the gentle slope of her upper chest. She carefully pries his fingers away and modestly readjusts her blouse.

"Colic," the woman says.

"Just tired," my mother replies.

"Colic," the woman says.

My mother begins to pace the room, jogging my brother up and down in hopes of enticing him to sleep. She has no such luck. The woman raises her voice over the sound of my brother's tantrum. She tells my mother they will take us to see the parsonage tomorrow afternoon. It is a modest two-bedroom home less than a half-mile from the church. The previous pastor's wife did not like it, but the walls have since been painted—yellow in the living room, orange in the kitchen, and green in the dining room—and new curtains hung, colored accordingly. The carpet in the living room—a beige shag—has been ripped out and replaced with carpet—beige shag—that had been sitting for several years in the garage of another deacon.

"Not the best, but cheap," the woman says.

Water pressure throughout the house is low, the steps to the back door need to be repaired, and the roof needs to be replaced. It leaks badly whenever the rain comes from the north. The oven works, but three of the four coils on the stove don't. The refrigerator is in the basement; the freezer on the front porch. The hot water heater needs to be replaced, the front porch enclosed, and the windows weather-proofed. The man who lives next door can't be trusted. He was arrested once for doing things with a little boy.

"They say he's fine now," the woman says.

My mother sees me sliding along the wall, angling toward the open doorway. She furrows her brow and tightens her lips, stares and waits for me to look back. When I do, she slowly and firmly says my name, and I hesitate, look toward the woman who casts a sidelong glance in my direction, but just keeps talking—she's moved on to the Ladies Missionary Society—then I continue toward the door.

It meets every Tuesday at 10 A.M. in the fellowship hall in the basement. Usually they stay until 11:30. They roll bandages, collect nonperishable items and make quilts to send overseas. Every week they choose a different missionary that the church supports, and they write a letter of encouragement. Coffee is mandatory—whoever makes it, usually the pastor's wife when they have a pastor's wife, has to arrive early to turn on the coffeepot—and sometimes someone will bring pastries.

When my mother catches up to me, I am well down the hall, aiming for the base of the steps, ready to climb. She bends at the waist to snag me, securing my brother with one hand, and grips my upper arm with the other. I scream as if I've been scalded by a hot iron. She firmly steers me back toward the nursery, the soles of my shoes tapping against the gray cement floor.

There is a need for piano players. The woman used to play herself, for many years, in fact. "But the old hands just ain't what they used to be," she says.

The organ hasn't been touched in months. The choir needs leadership—they sing "The Old Rugged Cross" every Sunday. Last year, the Christmas pageant forgot to include the baby Jesus, and Easter services were canceled because everyone was going to be out of town. No one wants to be in charge of the nursery schedule, and something needs to be done about the children during the morning service—they're always talking and crying and disturbing those who are trying to listen to the sermon.

My mother hunts through the diaper bag to find a Band-Aid. There is a floor burn on my knee from where I tripped and fell when I tried to break away from her grip as we came back into the nursery. I have thrown myself prostrate onto the floor.

The previous pastor's wife did not like being a hostess. She never invited people over to the parsonage. She didn't listen to advice, didn't appreciate people stopping by unannounced, and she was never willing to listen when someone had a problem.

"I guess it just wasn't her gift," the woman says.

Gossip is a problem. Mrs. Deleweather is the worst. Florence Ambla has cancer. Lucas Tootum has a herniated disk. And the daughter of someone named Della is pregnant.

"Had to drop out of school," the woman whispers.

My mother drops the diaper bag, nearly drops my brother, and pulls me away from the electrical socket in the wall. She yanks the penny from my hand and swats her hand across my butt. I scream—as if she's broken my pelvis.

"I hope," the woman says, "that isn't the kind of dress you'd wear on a Sunday morning."

Upstairs in the paneled room just off the auditorium, the men gathered around the table ask my father questions concerning church doctrine.

Do you believe in the sufficiency of Christ's blood atonement on the cross and his bodily resurrection three days later? Do you believe in salvation by grace and grace alone? The Virgin birth? A literal six-day, God-breathed creation? Do you believe that all scripture is given by inspiration of God, and is profitable for doctrine, for reproof, for correction, for instruction in righteousness? Do you believe in baptism by immersion? The imminent return of Christ? A pre-tribulation, pre-millennial rapture? The priesthood of the believer? The independence of the local church? Eternal security? A literal, physical hell?

My father wears a dark suit.

The woman's arms are held wide and she beckons for me with her brown splotched hands—alternately extended, then drawn toward her body—like she's guiding a small plane down the tarmac. Across the room at the base of the crib, I watch intently, but hold my ground, sock-covered feet planted as firmly as a 19-month-old can manage. One hand tugs absentmindedly at the diaper beneath my soft cotton pants, the other hooks securely around a leg of the crib for balance. This is the position respective of each other that Mrs. Brubaker and I will maintain for the next decade.

"Independent type, isn't he?" the woman says.

"Yes. He is. I think they're both going to be that way."

"Is it genetic? Their independence, I mean."

"I don't know," my mother says. "I suppose so."

My brother lies still in the crib, my mother mindful of a cracked wooden slat that will need to be replaced. The whole thing will need to be replaced. She is seated on the floor, legs tucked modestly beneath her. She had been directing my construction of a Lincoln Log house until I abandoned the project in protest of her artistically stifling suggestions. My initial protests were verbal, of the highest decibel possible.

"My children are the independent types," the woman says. "Independence isn't always such a good thing."

My mother attempts a half-hearted smile, uncertain of how to interpret the last comment. To Mrs. Brubaker, independence, my mother will soon learn, is never a good thing.

The woman tells my mother of her own children—there are two, a daughter and a son. She had always hoped her daughter would marry a preacher, had looked forward to grandchildren.

"But she didn't marry a preacher," the woman says. "Though I suppose it's for the best she didn't."

There is bitterness in the woman's voice, and my mother does not rush to soothe it.

The woman explains, in hushed tones, as if afraid someone will overhear, that her daughter is divorced, has been divorced for several years now. She claimed her husband abused her—not physically, but emotionally—and this is something the woman still cannot understand. She had married the son of her best friend in the church, a young man who had grown up side-by-side her daughter practically from birth. They were in the nursery at the same time. The marriage lasted less than two years, and the couple had been separated for nearly a year before Mrs. Brubaker and her husband were even aware there were problems in the marriage.

"She just gave up. 'For better or worse,' I kept saying, but she wouldn't listen. She had her own ideas by then and our ways had become 'old-fashioned.' That's what she said. Old-fashioned. The ways of God, I told her, are never old-fashioned."

Mother inquires about the son. He has moved to Florida. Joined a Pentecostal church. He calls on the first Sunday of every month, but when her husband tries to show him the error of his ways, starts quoting scripture—the same scripture every month—her son becomes angry and hangs up.

"How old are you?" the woman asks my mother.

"Twenty-four."

"And how long have you been married?"

"Nearly three years."

"Why did you marry your husband?" the woman asks.

My mother is slow to answer. Not because she does not know, but because of the forwardness of the question. Something so personal.

"Because I love him," she says, stating what she hopes is obvious.

"Did you know he was going to be a preacher when you met?"

"No. But it's something that we've talked about a lot. It's something to which we both feel led. Full-time ministry, I mean."

With room for herself finally in the conversation, my mother tells the woman about the desire she shares with my father to minister in a small town, to reach the lost for Christ, to raise their own family in a manner that would be pleasing onto the Lord. She wants to impress, to appear wise and mature beyond her years, full of hope and promise. She tells the woman how much she enjoys being a mother and how she is learning to appreciate every day with each child—they grow so fast. She tells the woman of the long drive, of the anxiety she and her husband have had for this weekend, the possibility of the beginning it may represent. She is telling the woman of the joy she takes from working with people, of being involved in their lives at the point of their needs, when she is abruptly interrupted.

"Don't expect people to love you," the woman says.

My mother pauses. The woman has stopped rocking in the chair and leans forward, hands clasped in her lap, her eyes firmly upon my mother.

"They'll love your husband. They won't love you."

Upstairs in that paneled room, just off the auditorium, my father addresses the role of the church in today's society.

We need prayer back in school. We need to teach teen-agers to wait until they're married to have sex. Rock music is the most powerful tool the devil has in his arsenal to reach youth today. Men should look like men and women should look like women. Co-ed housing on college campuses is a sin. Television numbs the mind. Hollywood pollutes it. Alcohol poisons the soul. Dancing creates lustful thoughts. Gambling steals from God. The rising divorce rate and the proposed Equal Rights Amendment will destroy our biblically based conception of the family. Vietnam must not fall into Communist hands. The Iron Curtain must be rent in two. Madelyn Murray-O'Hare is not the anti-Christ, but the Pope could be.

These are the end times.

"I don't envy you," the woman says.

My mother doesn't know how to respond, so leans over to whisper in my ear, but I'm quiet now and so she has nothing to say to me either. At first my mother thinks the woman is talking about being a young mother, having these two kids climbing all over, demanding this and demanding that, always crying and shouting and screaming, so completely dependent upon her.

"She was young. Like you," the woman says. "Had three small children. They would always sit together in the front row on the piano side. Those children were always so well behaved, just darling, the boys in their little suits and ties, looking like miniature versions of their father. And the little girl. What a doll. In those pink frilly dresses and tiny saddle shoes."

It had been the middle of winter. From thin metal hangers on the coat racks in the foyer, heavy wool coats hung, melted snow pooling in small puddles on the tile floor below, collecting around boots and rubber shoe covers and fallen knitted mittens. The pale wooden pews in the auditorium were filled—families taking up entire rows—and the hymnals were new, the bindings still taut and fresh. The handsome young preacher wore a dark suit with a white shirt, a dark tie knotted tightly against his starched collar. They said he had played football in college, and as he stood behind the pulpit, he still had the lean physique of a halfback. He began his sermon as he always did—with a reading of scripture, then prayer. There was nothing particularly notable about the beginning. Just another Sunday morning sermon. But after several minutes, a few in the congregation realized that he had stopped referring to his notes, that he was apparently just saying whatever was on his mind, quoting scripture and encouraging the congregation to forgive one another. And then he began to weep. There, standing behind the pulpit, he just burst into tears. After a few moments, he stopped trying to speak, bowed his head and gripped the sides of the pulpit with both hands.

"I remember looking toward her," the woman says, "and she was leaning forward uncertainly, as if she was deciding if she should go forward to the pulpit to see what might be the matter. She hesitated. We all waited. And then he gathered himself and stood tall again in the pulpit.

"And that's when he told the congregation that he had been having an affair with a woman who isn't my wife—that's the exact phrase he used; I still remember it clearly. A woman who isn't my wife. He was no longer weeping, just reciting the facts, you might say. The affair had been ongoing for a year and the woman had become pregnant and he knew he needed to take responsibility for the child and seek the church's forgiveness. He said he felt that he couldn't go on as our pastor if we couldn't forgive him, and he was standing before us to beg for our forgiveness. Like David, he said. And then he read from one of the Psalms."

His wife had never even suspected he was having an affair. It was a woman who had first come to her husband seeking help for her own marriage.

"I don't know how long he went on for that morning," the woman says, "talking about his sin and the need to seek and to grant forgiveness. But through the whole thing his wife just sat there in the front row, her back straight and firm, looking straight ahead to the pulpit, not looking back over her shoulder to see how we were responding, not a hint of waver. And there were the three kids all in a row beside her, prim and proper as could be. So well behaved. That's what I remember about them. They were always so well behaved."

When the service ended, the pastor's wife walked to the back of the church as she always did, and she stood beside her husband and shook hands with the departing congregation, which filed slowly through the center doors, firmly shaking the hand of the pastor and offering him the forgiveness he sought and wishing him strength for the coming days. They would pray for him. They would lift him before God for grace and peace. They would see him through the dark shadow of the valley through which he must pass.

The following Friday in the middle of the night, the young pastor's wife left the parsonage and walked the half-mile to the downtown bridge that joined the two halves of town. The river below was half-frozen over with ice. Schoolchildren found her body the next morning.

"What that must have done to her children," the woman says. "If only she had turned to God."

She shakes her head.

"He remained pastor of the church for five years after his wife's death," the woman says. "He eventually married the woman with whom he'd had the affair. She never sat in the front row though. It wouldn't have seemed right."

Upstairs in that paneled room, just off the auditorium, the coffee has turned cold. These are the questions now asked of my father. According to your understanding of scripture, what is the proper role of the wife? According to your understanding of scripture, what is the meaning of submission when it says that a wife should submit to her husband as unto the Lord? According to your understanding of scripture, should the wife work outside the home? According to your understanding of scripture, what is the proper role of women in the church? Should women serve in leadership capacities within the church? Should women be permitted to wear slacks inside the church? Do you permit your wife to wear make-up? Immodest clothing? Two-piece bathing suits? Excessive jewelry?

No one asks my father if he loves his wife.

When my father appears in the doorway of the nursery, he is accompanied by an overweight man with ruddy, wind-burned cheeks who wears a wine red sport coat with brass buttons and tennis ball green slacks. The day Mrs. Brubaker finally succumbs to cancer, surrounded by family on the second floor of their farmhouse, her husband will still be wearing the same combination.

My father lifts me from the floor, presses me above his head. I look down at him and he looks up at me and we both smile. Mother knows it has gone well for my father in the paneled room upstairs, that he has found the men in the suits agreeable and that they have found him young, but intelligent and serious and devoted and theologically correct.

Behind him, several more members of the board of deacons wait to take my parents to a local diner for coffee. They have offered us the option of spending the evening at the Brubakers' farm or bedding down at a local motel. My mother and father have decided beforehand that they would desire the privacy of a motel if it was offered, a chance to compare notes and build strategy for the morning when our family would take the stage to do its little holy pony show for the church. My father would preach—something convicting, but in a non-threatening way. My mother would be charming and graceful—but not artificially so. I would sit calmly beside my mother on the piano bench and be well behaved. My brother would simply giggle and coo, inspiring in the way only an infant can. There would be a potluck dinner after the morning service, a chance to meet-and-greet and shake hands, and then a brief respite at someone's home late in the afternoon before doing it all over again in the evening. Then there would be the six-hour drive home through the winter rain to the steady rnt . . . rnt . . . rnt of the windshield wipers, arriving home at two in the morning, hoping that this was the beginning and not another dead end.

If my mother were telling this story, this is how it would end.

Just over a month later, my father delivers his first sermon as pastor of the First Baptist Church of Paradise, Michigan. My mother plays the piano and sits in the front row with me beside her. My brother spends the hour in the nursery in the hands of strangers and doesn't shed a single tear. It will be the first of many sermons my father will deliver to the congregation in Paradise in the nearly 20 years he will serve as its pastor, 20 years that will fill with births and deaths, marriages and divorces, people moving in and people moving on. Three more children—two daughters and a third son—will join our family and all will grow up to be big and strong.

The congregation will grow until a new auditorium must be built to contain us all. My father will baptize each of his children in nearby Swan Creek. Summers will fill with vacation Bible school, scripture memory contests, and camp. My father will become a respected leader in the community, and everyone will always say that my mother does not look her age. My parents will spend their 10th anniversary in Israel, their 20th in Greece.

There will be many other memorable moments, some good, some not so good. My mother, if she were telling this story, would say they were mostly good.

But my mother isn't telling this story, and so it's not going to end the way she would end it. Instead, it will end like this.

It is that cold, wet, February night when my father still seemed more like a college kid than a preacher, and my mother still thought of herself more as a woman than as a wife. She is in bed beside my father, who is asleep, in the darkness of the motel room. My brother is cradled in a bassinet that one of the deacon's wives has loaned us, and I am curled up in the space between my parents. My father's Bible and his notes for the morning sermon are open on the small table near the door, and outside the rain has turned to snow and the roads have turned to ice.

My mother cannot sleep. She keeps replaying the conversation in her mind.

We are in the diner—three deacons and their wives, my father, my mother, my brother and I—crowded around a Formica-topped table that is littered with empty coffee cups, crumpled napkins, spoons and small puddles of spilled cream and milk. The conversation is loud and boisterous, filled with laughter and praise and the sense that something good has begun. Everyone knows that no one should say anything yet, nothing is official, but Mr. Brubaker asks anyway, asks my father if he'd accept the call if the church extended an offer.

"Well, that's not a decision I would make by myself," my father says.

"But, of course," says Mr. Brubaker. "You'd pray about it, certainly. For the Lord's leading."

My mother, who is sitting across from my father between the wives of two deacons she has only just met, waits for my father to clarify his statement, to say that he wouldn't make the decision without consulting her, that it would be a mutual decision of husband and wife, of their future. Together. With the Lord's leading, of course.

But my father says nothing of the sort. Merely nods his head in agreement. Wives, submit yourselves unto your own husbands, as unto the Lord. For the husband is the head of the wife, even as Christ is the head of the church. Mr. Brubaker raises his coffee cup in a mock toast.

"To the Lord's leading," he says in all earnestness.

All around the table, the adults reach for their coffee cups with solemn faces that give way to grins and laughter as cups are clanked, and the last of the pot drained.

In the motel room, my mother turns her head toward my father. She can't quite see him in the darkness, but she can hear his breathing, sense his presence. She reaches across my limp body, allows her hand to hover close to my father's shoulder, close enough to feel the heat rising from his skin. She considers waking him, to ask him to clarify his statement for her. But instead she settles back into her pillow and closes her eyes. In that moment, she resents my father. This is where it begins.

Punitive Damages

will have fifteen minutes. That's how much time they give me to speak. They place me on an airplane in Marquette (it's February, 77 inches of snow on the ground, 240 now for the season) and fly me 3,000 miles to an island in the Caribbean, where it's 80 degrees every day. They house me in a hotel suite large enough for my entire extended family, but it's just me on this trip, me and the marble hot tub, the panoramic view of blue-green waters. They provide for all my meals (flying fish, fried plantains, rice, fresh mango) and drinks (it's an open bar), and arrange for guided tours and opportunities to snorkel along the reefs. Every night another calypso band with dancing and beautiful women. All for four days and four nights, and then they fly me home again, 3,000 miles, two layovers, and an invitation to return again soon. In exchange I have those fifteen minutes. I remind myself not to speak too fast. They will use an interpreter for those who do not speak English.

Every month now it is like this. Last month, Bonn, Germany. Next month, Brisbane, Australia. Always the same scene. In Bonn, twenty-five minutes. In Brisbane, ten.

The Caribbean sun cooks my skin, and the water from the pool evaporates and the sunscreen melts away. I turn over onto my back and do a mini-stomach crunch, the muscles in my abs tightening. I lift the cocktail glass from the side of the pool and take another sip. I shouldn't drink too much alcohol in this sun. It isn't healthy. But still I wave toward the bartender—one more please—and then lie back and close my eyes.

When I feel a hand on my shoulder, I abruptly sit up. Though it takes a few moments for my eyes to adjust to the overwhelming brightness of the afternoon sun, I recognize the voice—the director of the conference, a professor of ethics at St. George's Medical School. He's a generous, portly man, who keeps reminding me that he grew up in Wisconsin and loves to call his mother in Fond du Lac and tell her the temperature here. He apologizes for the interruption and asks if there's anything I will require later that evening when I speak. I tell him, no, I'm fine, just tell me when and where. Then he introduces a woman that I realize has been standing beside him the entire time. I quickly stand, brushing my hands across my swim trunks to make sure nothing bulges inappropriately.

I know her story, it was in *Time* magazine and on the evening network news, but I listen anyway as the director of the conference, by means of introduction, says, " . . . whose daughter died . . . whose son died. . . ." This has become our identity. We are the parents of the deceased. We are the wronged, the damaged, the unfulfilled.

She extends her hand and I take it. Soft, smooth skin. I examine her more closely. She wears a modest floral print dress—conservative, tasteful, falling just below the knees—a watch with a gold band and a pink plastic bracelet that I imagine belonged to her daughter. She seems too young to be the mother of the deceased.

"I'm sorry," I say.

"Thank you," she says.

My eyes meet hers. She reaches out her hand and places it upon my bare shoulder. Her hand feels cool in the tropical air and a surge of electricity ripples through my body, running just beneath the surface of the skin.

"We should get together and exchange notes," I say.

She nods. "I'd like that. Very much."

The director touches her elbow and says they need to keep moving. She's only just arrived, the plane was delayed, and they need to get her settled into her room. I watch as she turns. I admire the flex in her calves as she walks in her black pumps, see her hips shift beneath her skirt, follow the gentle slope of her neck, the pale skin there.

When they're gone, I sit at the edge of the pool, feet kicking beneath the surface of the water. I drain the last of my rum punch, and smile. I can barely restrain myself. Two years ago I'd never been west of the Mississippi, never outside the borders of the United States, and now I'm traveling the world. All because I put my son on an airplane, and when he came back, he was dead.

Here's what I say in my fifteen minutes: I loved my son. Nothing can ever take his place. I miss those late afternoons in the backyard when the golden sun filtered through the leaves on the maple trees as we played catch, the baseball arcing back and forth from hand to glove. He had blue eyes and dirty blonde hair. He was always running into things—poles, end tables, chicken coops. He wanted to be a rock star—a ROCK STAR, I say. He wanted to be an astronaut, an astrophysicist, an astronomer. He was a hero to his little sister (how she misses him). He loved *The Simpsons,* knew all the episodes, could do all the voices on command ("*Aye, karumba!*"). He loved to perform, loved to make people laugh, and we were always laughing when we were in his presence. If I could reverse time, I would never have driven my son to the airport to take the plane to Boston. We would have overslept. Changed our minds. Gone to Big Bay de Noc instead. To camp. To fish. To talk father-to-son. I miss these talks, I say. He taught me so much.

And then, when the silverware rests quietly on the table, the baked brie and stuffed cod now forgotten, I add: For the purposes of wrongful death suits, the experts have determined the value of a human life. It rises every year with inflation. They have told me how much my son's life was worth. That's how much we received for his death. It isn't enough. It could never be enough. We need new laws. Better enforcement. Medicine must not be about profits. Healing is not a business. Our children are not guinea pigs. He was my son. I loved my son.

When I finish, they stand and applaud, every single person at every single table. There are tears and clenched fists and the biting of lips, a righteous anger and a new determination. Then they reach for their checkbooks, sign petitions, and promise action.

When she finishes, she is weeping. Two months ago, her three-year-old daughter died because of a failure of the doctors to follow the law. They gave her medication that had not yet been fully approved, and the little girl had an allergic reaction to it and died. Everyone watches silently as she steps down from the dais, and then they are on their feet to applaud this act of courage. They are doctors and nurses, medical ethicists and politicians on junkets. There is a celebrity spokesperson—a second-tier Hollywood actor—and the island's Governor-General. They think they understand what it is like to lose a child, but they don't. Watching someone else's child die is not the same as watching your own child die.

By the time I reach her, a human wall has formed around her. I don't know what people think they can say, but no one ever says anything that should be said. When she sees me, she smiles weakly and I smile back. We are co-conspirators, the parents of the deceased. I press through the crowd, and she sees me again and moves my way. Even away from the dais, the glare of the lights follows her. She wears a modest black dress with a gold herringbone necklace, gold earrings, and that pink plastic bracelet. She's worked hard to look beautiful for this night. I take her hand and lean my lips to her ear and say, "Let me get you out of here, get you some air."

We walk together through the foyer of the hotel and into the street. The cool night air refreshes the body and I loosen the tie I always wear when I give these speeches, a tie my son gave to me as a Father's Day gift a few years ago. Within a matter of seconds, we are away from the hotel, away from the conference, away from the tables of wine and rum and bananas and mangos and fish. We walk side-by-side in the narrow street, the sound of the Caribbean lapping against the cement wall of the *carenage*. We are alone as we walk past the island shops and businesses, all but a small café closed until morning.

She tells me about her daughter and I tell her about my son—the liver disorder that he controlled with daily medication, how we volunteered him for trials of a new treatment, something that would improve not only his life, but that of others for years to come. She tells me about the mistakes that were made with her daughter and of the absent father who didn't even attend the funeral, and I tell her how the research team misled me and how I misled them, and the finger-pointing that followed. She tells me about growing up in Iowa and I tell her about my father's work in the copper mines of northern Michigan. Then we talk about the conference and the people who are there and the reasons they bring people like us to speak about our experiences. I tell her about Europe and Australia and Japan.

Eventually she asks, "How much did they give you?"

"I'm not at liberty to say."

"A lot?"

"Everything we asked for."

"How did you know how much to ask for?"

I shrug. "There's a formula," I say. "Lawyers."

"Do you ever feel guilty?" she asks. "For taking all that money. Like the money could somehow make it right."

"No," I say. "For what they did, they should pay. Somehow. Some way. Someone has to get that money."

I allow the back of my hand to brush against hers, but she steps away, folding her arms across her chest.

"Ask for more than you've ever imagined," I say. "You can never ask for too much."

Our footsteps echo against the cement walkway. Two teen-age boys rush past, a late evening game of tag.

"Sometimes I wish my daughter would've never been born," she says, her eyes following the boys as they disappear behind us. "It would be so much easier to live without this. I used to think of myself as happy."

"You will be happy again," I assure her. She smiles, then, for a moment, closes her eyes.

After losing a child, there is denial and anger and guilt and then punitive damages.

From my room, I call my wife. She has remained at home to tend to the rest of our children for whom life continues unabated. School. Little League baseball. Violin lessons. They will all go to college now. It will all be paid for. Our friends believe our son's death brought my wife and me back together again and maybe my wife believes the same, but it was only the settlement that kept us together, the sheer mass of money and a mutual desire not to waste it on divorce lawyers, the hangers-on, and the friends that had suddenly appeared on our doorstep. We could afford to live together now, in a house large enough to provide each of us with our own space, to move in a world large enough to give us our own sense of self.

We don't talk long. There isn't much to be said that she hasn't heard before—of the accommodations, of the conference schedule, of my mission here on behalf of our son. What she hasn't heard I have no intention of sharing—not tonight, not when I get back home, not ever. Besides it's late and she wants to work on the kitchen in the morning before she goes to yoga. The kitchen is her pet project. Her therapist told her she needed to give herself projects, because life would continue even without our son, and now she needs a Palm Pilot to organize basic household chores. She spoke of our son once at a local Rotary luncheon, but it went so poorly— she kept stumbling over her words, losing her place in her notes, forgetting key details, saying, "I don't know," to questions—that she decided to leave the public advocacy to me. When we hang up, I call room service and order a ham sandwich and a local beer. I almost call Leslie, the woman who lost her daughter, to join me, but I realize I forgot to ask her room number, so I watch Brazilian soccer highlights on Telemundo, then fall asleep.

I awake at four in the morning to find myself erect. I have been dreaming, but before I can recall a moment of the dream, it is gone. I masturbate until I cum, it doesn't take long, thinking about Leslie. There was a place on the *carenage,* between a business supply store and a camera shop, where I thought we could have done it if she'd been willing. Maybe tomorrow, I think.

On these trips, there are always women. Some are women who have lost their own children. Some are academics, doctors, medical school students. Some not much older than my son would be. We strike a conversation in the lounge or the hallway or near the front of the auditorium, she just one of many crowded around me to offer sympathy, thanks, apologies, a business card, a brochure, a book proposal. There is eye contact, a smile, a touch of the hand—to hand, to shoulder, to hip. It lingers. She offers a chance to get away from the crowd, the noise, the glare of the spotlight, the demands, the grief. So we leave, heads down, deep into our own stories, and we have drinks, maybe dinner at a nearby restaurant where the service is mediocre and the food its equal. We take a long walk, along the beach, through the downtown, past shops that closed at five, until one of us says, it's cold or it's humid or it's hot or it looks like rain, and then we some-how, always, find our way to her room or to mine—once to an alcove of orange trees, once to an unoccupied conference room, the tables still cov-ered with cake crumbs and soiled linen napkins—and all conversation ceases as we undress, revealing ourselves to each other in a way that brings more comfort than shame, more relief than guilt. In the darkness of the room, we feel less naked than we feel in the convention hall. We forget death and we fuck until she collapses in tears beside me, the guilt and the shame and the loss and the orgasm surging through her body in alternat-ing waves, and I stare at the ceiling and think not of my son as she wishes to believe, but of her body and her breasts and her lips and how she com-pares to the other women with whom I have slept—in these recent months and in all those years gone by before my son died, before my son was born. At the end, sometimes in the middle of the night, sometimes in the morn-ing, we dress, and there is a long, lingering hug and she holds tightly to me as though her departure she cannot bear, and then she is gone.

The following morning I find myself in a purple-and-gold van that rush-es through the streets of St. George's to the tin sounds of calypso: bells and whistles, steel drums and shouts of bacchanal. My breakfast of ham and fish and fresh papaya juice sways from one side of my stomach to the other. Our driver, a large black man in cut-off denim shorts, a well-washed black Bob Marley T-shirt, and a cotton Muslim skull cap, bounces up and down in his seat and hits the accelerator and then the brake and then the accelerator again, tapping the horn to warn pedestri-ans, human and otherwise, to move out of the way. I cling to the armrest of the seat behind our driver—he says to call him Senator—as over the rattle of the calypso he narrates the history of the island and its people, shouting and pointing to various landmarks as we zip by. The House of Parliament, Scots Kirk Presbyterian Church, Market Square, the Sendall Tunnel. In-between bits of narrative, he sings along to the tape, his voice thick with the sounds of the island, slapping his bare palms against the steering wheel, the roof of the van, his own muscular thighs, leaving us to distinguish the shops from the churches from the warehouses from the government buildings.

This was Leslie's idea. She'd found me in the hotel lobby, butter still on my lips, and persuaded me to join her for a guided tour of the island. I loathed the prospect of an island tour, but she stood close to me and begged me. "I have to get out of here," she said. When we found ourselves Senator's only customers, he assured us that we would have his full attention. Whatever our desires, he would make certain they were fulfilled. Food. Wine. Music. "Women," he said, looking at me. "Men," he said, looking at Leslie. "This is my island and whatever I have is yours," he said, "so think of our island as home."

Now Leslie slides back and forth across the vinyl seat, trying to take pictures with a digital camera, as Senator whips the van around tight corners and down narrow streets. As Senator speaks, the history of the island and the history of his life become intertwined and inseparable, each a necessary part of the other—the island, Senator, its wars, his wars, its women, his women. He studied in Britain before the invasion, returned to open his own import/export business, has four wives (only one legal) and eleven children. He claims to have slept with over 700 women. He plays in a calypso band, a band everybody loves—everybody loves Senator—and when his own band isn't performing, he mc's for other bands, develops their talents, shows them how to mix the old with the new. He wants to run for parliament, he wants to be a politician. "It's all about tourism," he says. He has a thousand ideas to improve the island, to help his people. "Being in politics is sort of like being in a calypso band," he says. "Lots of noise to make people happy."

Every so often Leslie hollers for Senator to stop and he obliges, stops right in the middle of whatever street we happen to be on, everyone behind us honking their own horns. Leslie jumps out of the van and makes a beeline for some cramped shop or vendor's cart. Even as she hurries across the street, I am embarrassed for her. She looks like a tourist in her khaki capri pants and white blouse, Teva sandals, and sunglasses that are too large for her face. She carries a small backpack, not a real backpack, a pack large enough to hold a pocketbook and a set of keys, if the keys are few enough and unimportant enough. When she returns to the van, tiny knick-knacks fill her backpack. She says she wants to find the perfect memento by which to remember this trip, but her tastes run to kitsch, cheap souvenirs designed solely for women like Leslie—nutmeg key chains, cricket bat magnets, tiny plastic bags of spice. Eventually, she begins to drag me with her and she holds up objects and asks my opinion, dickers with me in a good-natured way, defending her choices, and then ignores me and pays too much. The streets are cluttered with people and panhandlers who recognize us as Americans and I begin to regret the decision to join her. I contemplate a headache or a forgotten forum, anything that could allow me to graciously excuse myself from the jostling crowds and the stares reserved for foreigners. But then she slips her arm into mine and pulls my arm against her side. She gives me a big smile, all white teeth and blue sky, her skin soft, her body firm. I urge myself on, knowing the day will have its rewards.

For lunch, Senator takes us to a small café along the *carenage,* a neatly kept establishment with fresh bread and espresso and a view of the harbor through the plate-glass front wall. Leslie orders a salad with greens, breadfruit, papaya and bananas, and I choose a Genoa salami sandwich on French bread with a latté. Senator assures us the café produces the best bread on the island, though he says there's a bakery in neighboring Carriacou for which he'd offer his first-born son.

We take our time in the café, gathering our cue from those around us. No one seems to be in a hurry, the late morning sun warm and inviting. Senator continues to unfurl the island's history for us, its role as a British colony, the Fedon rebellion, the development of the spice industry, and the region's passion for cricket. And because we are Americans, because he knows the things we want to hear, he directs our attention to the view of the harbor from our chairs just inside the café. When we look to the northeast, we see Fort George, an aging seventeenth-century structure that now serves as the headquarters of the island police, the place, says Senator, where they killed Bishop. He points to the northwest, and we see the bombed-out remains of an old hotel, still charred and gutted from that night back in '83 when U.S. warplanes swept low over the city and dropped their bombs and missiles, destroying the rebel headquarters (there, at the hotel, no money to repair it even after all these years) and the mental hospital, a targeting mistake that killed twelve Grenadians.

As he speaks, Senator becomes increasingly animated. He makes sweeping gestures with his hands. He talks about the president who believed in UFOs, the revolution that removed him from power, and the reforms that followed. He talks about the airport and the Cubans, a charismatic leader—"if Bishop were still alive, no one else could rule this island"—and things that went wrong. He gives names, dates, and places, but soon it all runs together and I can't keep track of who was who or how or when or why, and so I just nod and sip my latté and place my hand onto Leslie's knee. Senator assumes that we remember as he remembers, that those days when Grenada was shoved onto the international stage are permanently etched into our knowledge, right alongside the American Revolution and Pearl Harbor and the assassination of John F. Kennedy. I can't bring myself to tell him that I remember nothing of the intervention—save that Reagan was President and we came and we left and maybe a few people died. That's all I know. I don't know why we came or what has happened since or why it should matter that I don't.

We all want to believe our grief is unique, that our experience with death somehow sets us apart from the rest of the world. We have lost our children, we have lost our leaders, we have lost our revolutions, and in our grief, we believe we have been given some secret knowledge, an insight into the way the world works that is hidden from the blind. But we are not unique. The manner of death may seem unusual, a novelty, but death spares no one and visits itself upon all that walk this world.

Outside the café, small wooden rowboats painted brilliant oranges and greens, reds and blues line the inside of the harbor. The water gently laps against the concrete wall. Schoolchildren in uniforms (white blouses and plaid skirts for the girls; white oxford shirts and navy blue slacks for the boys) walk along the *carenage*. They peer through the windows and into the café. Leslie stares blankly in return.

At first everything reminds you of your loss: another child, a doctor, a medical clinic, a toy, a game, the sound of metal clicking against wood, the smell of a diaper, the sun, the moon. But eventually it fades and though others will remind you ("How are you doing?" they ask. "I'm sorry," they say), soon it's just another story you tell, like the first day of kindergarten or the time you spilled chili on your wife's white dress. At appropriate times, you tell it and you learn to tell it well, and those who must listen respond as they should.

Senator assures us that most of the people were glad the Americans came. "Someone had to come," he says. But then he realizes neither of us is listening, and so he becomes silent and we all sit quietly in the café, lost in our own thoughts.

In the countryside, we do not travel far between stops. Rum shops—small wooden shacks with a few weather-beaten wooden stools outside and an inside back wall lined with bottles of beer, like lemonade stands for grown-ups—litter the narrow two-lane road that winds along the leeward coast. We seem to stop at every one. Everyone knows Senator, and even early in the afternoon, the drinks flow. Senator downs his with ease, slapping dominoes on the upturned top of a wooden barrel, talking trash to his opponent until the last piece is played, and then empties his bottle, slaps the barkeep on the back, and leads us back into the van. Leslie only sips her drinks and I take to drinking hers as well as mine. At the first couple stops, we pay for our own drinks, but soon everything is on the house—either at Senator's behest or from the rum shopkeeper's generosity. The beers are local and from nearby islands (Carib, Piton, Hairoun), the wines produced in adjacent fields, allowed to ferment in neighboring basements. The wines have handwritten labels and a cheap, grainy quality that lingers from one rum shop to the next.

At one stop, the barkeeper asks Leslie and me if we have come together, if this is our honeymoon. She smiles shyly and tells him we're not married, we're not even a couple, but he says, "That doesn't mean this can't be a honeymoon!" and pours us more drinks. We tell him we're from the States, and the barkeeper tells us he spent a year at a small college in the Midwest. "Too cold," he says. "And so was the weather!"

He laughs at his joke, and we indulge him with smiles. Then we thank him for the drinks and pile back into the van.

Senator pushes the van hard and it seems to float free of the earth as we crest small hills. In his seat, Senator sways to the calypso. This is his band and these are his songs and he is having a good time. Along the road, people shout his name—"Senator! Senator! Senator!"—waving frantically as they run for a moment beside us. Each time, Senator extends his long arm out the open window in greeting and taps the horn with the other.

We stop to examine petroglyphs along a coastal sea wall near Victoria, remnants of the Caribs. Most of the petroglyphs have been damaged, stolen, or destroyed by vandals and trophy hunters. When we drive past a refuse dump, just up the road from the petroglyphs, the garbage smoldering in the mid-afternoon sun, Senator shakes his head in embarrassment. "If Bishop were in charge," he says.

It is Danny, a fisherman from Moliniere, who tells Senator that he should take us to Sauteurs, to Caribs' Leap.

Senator nods. "A very spiritual place," he says. He takes a deep breath, then a sip of his wine. He stares off into the distance as though he's trying to see Caribs' Leap from here.

Danny smiles, then whispers, "Senator thinks every place is a spiritual place."

"It is!" Senator says.

Leslie asks Senator why it's such a spiritual place.

Danny answers. He explains how, in 1651, the Carib people revolted against a French force that sought to conquer the island's indigenous people and to take control of the island. But when the revolt failed, the Carib warriors' poisoned arrows and clubs no match for the French cannons and firearms, the French counterattacked and chased a band of forty Carib warriors across the island. The warriors fled for their lives until they came to the end of the island and the beginning of the sea. They were trapped. On one side were the French, prepared to subject the warriors to slavery or even worse. On the other side, a 130-foot cliff that dropped straight to the sea and to certain death.

"So they jumped," Danny says. "First one man and then the next and then the next and the next until there were none."

Everywhere we go, Leslie snaps pictures. She explains that she didn't take many pictures of her daughter. She always took it for granted that her daughter would be there until Leslie herself died, would be there for all time, and so she was always saving film. It was so damned expensive, the processing and the preserving and the framing. So now she has a digital camera and she takes pictures of everything. This is what frightens her the most—that one day she'll be unable to remember her daughter, unable to recall her face to memory, unable to remember the exact shade of her blue eyes.

After every few shots, she hands me the camera. On the tiny screen, I see again everything we just saw, only smaller and somehow with more vivid colors. She takes photos of the banana trees and the hibiscus and the spice vendors. She takes pictures of Senator with his favorite beer and she takes pictures of me with my arm raised to block my face. She takes photos of each of the rum shops and each of the barkeepers and of the other patrons, mostly men, almost all out of work or skipping work. She asks each of them for their names and she writes them down in a small notebook so she'll remember who they are. Some ask for copies of the photos and Leslie asks for their e-mail addresses, but the men do not have computers and they do not have e-mail addresses, and so they give her post office box numbers or street addresses, and she promises to send them prints as soon as she returns to the States.

Somewhere near Guayoye, we pass a woman carrying a child, wrapped in a linen cloth, two other small children—maybe four or five years old—walking close beside her on the gravel. Leslie sits upright as we near, then turns to follow the woman as Senator steers the van to the center of the road to give the woman clearance. Leslie's eyes hold the woman until the van takes the bend to the right and the woman disappears from view.

At our next stop, another rum shop, Leslie finishes her drink and asks Senator for another. Senator gives her a second drink and she finishes it and asks for another. Senator laughs and promises there will be more for her at the next stop. She tells Senator she used to love to drink, before her child was born, and that she gave it up when she had the child, not wanting anything to come between her and her child. Senator asks about her child, Alyssa, and then Leslie tells the story that appeared in *Time* magazine.

She stumbles through her story. It is still too fresh, the facts still slippery, the emotions not yet ordered. She tells the story from start to finish, gives too many details for the listener's sake—birthday gifts, a cat named Renaldo, a blue dress. Everything is still important to her now; she hasn't learned yet that we're only indulging her, that it's not her daughter's life, it's only her death that interests us. Soon she will learn what to include and what to leave out. The story will become more concise, more efficient. She will find the right phrases more quickly, those lines they'll remember months from now when they recall the story and repeat it to a friend or colleague or cousin. The sorrow will be what they remember. The loss of a child. How does anyone cope? She will understand that we don't want to live what she has lived. We only want to know enough to be glad it wasn't us.

We are drunk now. Senator pulls the van to the side of the road and leads the way down a narrow, rocky trail that emerges on a small, protected beach. He's shouting and encouraging us on as he strips out of his shorts and T-shirt and underwear, then runs into the surf, naked, his hard dark body glistening in the Caribbean sun. The water is tropical, greens and blues, coffee table beautiful, and I see her undressing, partially hidden by a gray, volcanic boulder, still a bit uneasy, not drunk enough yet for it all to come off. I begin to strip, my eyes on her, the white bra, the white panties, long legs heavy with childbirth, her belly heavier than I had imagined, and my heart nearly skips a beat. Then she is in the water and I am close behind, wearing only my boxers. The water is warm and the salt stings my eyes, the rocks beneath the surface sharp on my feet. I fall into the water, swim a few strokes, roll over onto my back, float, the water cradling me. I close my eyes and lie there, the sun warm on my skin. I think of my son, lying on his back in that hospital room, staring into the ceiling, the fluorescent lights, the antiseptic smell, the impending death. He did not know what was coming. My son closed his eyes and never opened them again.

When the phone rang, my wife answered it. They told her everything went wrong. Immediately. The body had rejected the treatment in a way and to a degree they had in no way anticipated. Lesions developed on his internal organs and they spread and swelled until the organs burst and ceased to function, a sort of nuclear meltdown inside his body. Now there was nothing they could do. She wept bitterly and I held her until she wore herself out, and then I called a lawyer. The doctors had told us it would be next to routine. They had assured us all the proper precautions would be taken. Within a week, we had filed the necessary papers and less than four months later we settled out of court for $11 million.

In the wake of our son's death, we determined our lives would change. We would work harder at our marriage; we would give more attention to our living children; and we would appreciate every moment of every day. Then in the wake of the settlement, we determined that nothing in our lives would change. We would live in the same house and drive the same cars and use the same snow-blower in the winter. In short, we would hold the same values as we had always held. We began with good intentions.

I hear Leslie screech and Senator laugh. I sit abruptly upright, water splashing over me, salt in my eyes, and I swing my arms and feel the water's resistance, and I swing my arms back and forth, and we are laughing and swinging and the spray of water feels good and we fall over drunk into the water and jump back up again until we're too tired to do this anymore and we force ourselves to the shore, like beached whales.

Senator insists the place will be packed in a matter of hours, bodies pulsing in the exotic air, the rhythms of calypso coursing through muscle tissue and bone marrow and blood cells until bodies and music are indistinguishable. But now, in the late afternoon, the dance hall is bare, the wooden floor empty, revealing center planks long stripped of the green paint that yet marks the hall's edges. The wooden window flaps are raised to allow what little tropical breeze exists to work its way from one side of the hall to the other. On the walls are dog-eared posters of bikini-clad Caribbean women, the logos of local beer distributors on prominent display. Behind the counter, bottles of rum and vodka and other hard liquors line the shelves. There's a cash register at one end of the counter and a small handwritten sign that reads, "Cash only. No tabs."

Senator slides a shot in front of me and says, "Here. Drink this."

It resembles soup more than a drink, thick and green. He pours himself a shot from a large plastic jug. There are no labels on the jug. The drink looks as though scooped from a sledge pit.

"It's called Under-the-Counter. A man's drink." Senator laughs. "'Tis what gives me my vitality, allows me to go all night long. How do you think I keep four wives happy?"

Senator grins, then lifts his own shot from the countertop, and in an instant the thick, gray-green liquid is gone. Senator purses his lips and I know he did not enjoy the drink. He only believed in it, the way Catholics believe in communion.

"What's in it?" I ask.

"Don't ask. It'll turn your stomach."

"One-hundred sixty-five proof," the woman behind the counter says.

I take my own shot glass, raise it to my lips, let my tongue touch its surface. Then I throw my head back and pour the thick liquid into my mouth, nearly gag, pull my head forward, and everything seems caught in between, in my mouth, in my throat, in the glass, and I throw my head back again, force myself to open my throat and let it go down. I choke and I gag and finally I'm able to swallow and swallow again and a third time and finally it's all gone, some of it on its way to my stomach, some of it on the countertop. Senator laughs.

"Never hesitate," he says. "He who hesitates is lost!"

Soon, the island tour has been forgotten and the conference has been forgotten and the panel discussions have been forgotten and we are sparring over Clinton and Lewinsky, sex and Puritanism, Carnival and Mardi Gras. We drink and we drink. Senator begins calling Leslie "my angel." I stare between the buttons of her blouse, the white silk brassiere cupping her full breast, and I stare at the nape of her neck, the long slope that I wish to kiss.

We wind our way around to Grenadian politics and Senator picks up where he left off an hour ago in the van. He rattles through his stump speech, tourism and bananas and education and more tourism. I've become his most ardent supporter, his American friend, his campaign manager. I volunteer to write his speeches, to raise his funds, to organize, organize, organize! "We'll take the message to the people! Senator for Senator! A mango in every pot!"

Senator roars at my attention, and soon I find myself balancing atop my chair, a fist raised, a revolutionary in Dockers, and I wave to an old man who sits at the far end of the bar, and in my most sincere, drunken voice, I ask him: "Would you, dear sir, cast your vote, your one precious God-given vote, for all that is good and just and right in the world, and cast it for our dear Senator?"

When the man says nothing, I feel Senator's hand tug at my pant leg.

"Sit down," Senator says. "You're making yourself a fool."

I laugh. I don't care. I'm a million miles from home. "Well," I say, "what is it, kind sir?"

The old man says, "If Bishop were alive, there be nobody else for my vote." He begins to talk in carefully measured tones about a young and charismatic revolutionary, a lawyer, barely thirty years old, and the overthrow of the old regime in a bloodless coup. I realize he's telling us the same story Senator told us at the café, of the days leading up to the U.S. intervention, of Grenada's fifteen minutes of international fame. How the movement split, the prime minister against the hard-line ideologues, how Bishop was placed under house arrest and jailed. He describes how, six days later, the people of Grenada rose up and freed Bishop from prison and carried him through the streets of St. George's—30,000 people, a gathering unlike any ever seen before or since.

"When the crowd reached the fort," he says, "those loyal to their commanders in the army attacked the people. They opened fire. No one knows how many died. Bishop and the members of his cabinet were rounded up and marched inside the fort, lined up against a cement wall, and shot."

The old man stares at Senator and Senator stares into his glass. He points to it and the woman behind the counter quickly refills it.

"Everyone involved was so young," the old man says. "Teenagers they were. Young men, hardly more than boys."

The old man stands, lays a pocketful of change on the counter alongside the empty bottle of beer.

"Even now people still remember who took whose side," he says. He nods to the woman behind the counter and she nods back in thanks.

When he's gone, Leslie announces that she has something to say. "I need to be honest," she says.

"Be honest," I say. "You're among friends."

I am seated now. We're all seated.

"I wasn't a very good mother."

"Bullshit," says Senator, and he slaps his hand on the counter. "You must be a wonderful mother. Clear as day. Anyone can see that."

She shakes her head back and forth.

"No. I failed my daughter. That's the bottom line. I wasn't a very good mother. I spanked her. All the time. I didn't do laundry enough. Sometimes I just collected soiled clothes from the floor of her room and placed them on her bed and told her to wear them again. I should have fed her better, but I was always cutting corners so I could go to a movie or buy a new sofa."

I extend my hand and place it on her shoulder, but find Senator's hand already there. His skin is thick and rough. I abruptly pull my hand back, wondering how long he had worked in the cane fields before he became a Calypso King. I wonder what his wives are doing today. I wonder what he tells them when he comes home.

Leslie leans into Senator's shoulder and I hear her softly weeping.

"There, there," Senator says. He gestures to the woman behind the counter with his free hand, and she places a box of tissues on the countertop. Leslie wipes a tissue against her cheek. I point to my shot glass and the woman looks at Senator, then fills my glass. This time I don't hesitate. This time, I barely taste it.

"My turn," I say. I stare at the countertop, arms folded, head down. Out of the corner of my eye, I can see Leslie turn her shoulders to see me. She still has Senator's full attention. His eyes are on the slope of her neck; his fingers massage her shoulder. His hand seems huge around her small, bird-like shoulder bones.

"My son's death is the best god-damned thing that's ever happened to me."

Leslie inhales sharply, then begins to cough. With the palm of his hand, Senator rubs her back in large circles.

"You don't mean that," she says.

I turn my eyes to her to allow her to see that I do mean it.

"A wake-up call, aye," Senator says. "A spiritual awakening. Brings you closer to God."

"No," I say. I do not want them to misunderstand. "Just the best god-damned thing that could've happened to me. Better than winning the lottery."

It becomes still inside the dance hall.

"Look at me! I'm in the fricking Caribbean! Lounging around the pool of some exclusive resort. Drinking all I can drink. Before all this, I never even made it to god-damn Detroit! I hated my life. Now look at me!"

I point to my shot glass. I want more. I'll drink all night now.

"Shit. This is the life. This is living."

Leslie wants to return now. It's been a long day. There's a panel discussion this evening in the auditorium, and if we hurry, she'll have time to shower and change, maybe even grab a bite to eat, get something solid in her stomach to absorb all this alcohol. Senator agrees. It'll be dark soon anyway, and the crazies take to the road after it gets dark, everyone done with work and nothing else to do but get drunk and wander into the road. But I don't want to hear any of this. I insist we finish the trip, finish the tour, drive to Sauteurs, to Carib's Leap, this spiritual place, this place of honor and dignity and death, see this god-damn place where forty men threw themselves off the cliff and onto the rocks below.

Senator is reluctant. It doesn't seem like such a good idea now—the enthusiasm gone. Leslie presses against Senator and he wraps his arm around her shoulder. She shivers though the air is still warm. Senator tries to convince me that it's not that big a deal, really, no one ever goes there, but this only heightens my interest, strengthens my demands. Finally Senator relents, assures Leslie it won't take long, and we pile back into the van.

As the day gives way to the dark, Senator drives the final half-hour in silence. We don't stop at any roadside rum shops and we see fewer and fewer people and when we do see someone they don't wave, they just stare as we pass.

When we reach Sauteurs, Senator parks the van in a small lot adjacent to a Catholic church and primary school. The shadows of gravestones and crucifixes stretch long across the cemetery grounds that lie between us and the cliff. The grounds are not well kept. The soil is rocky and overrun with weeds. It has been attended to, but not recently. A weather-beaten metal sign, rusted, its paint peeling, reads: Carib's Leap. An arrow points to a thin dirt path that cuts through the center of the cemetery.

"This is it?" I say. "This is fucking it?"

Senator says nothing. Leslie stares through the front windshield but makes no movement toward the door. I slide open the door and step outside, stumbling as my feet reach for the ground. I don't bother to close the door behind me, just start walking past the front of the van.

"How the hell do they expect anyone to find this place?" I holler back to Senator. "No wonder you have no tourism here."

I slap the signpost with my hand and hear it vibrate back and forth.

"Think of the possibilities," I holler. "Just think of the possibilities! A T-shirt stand! A coffeehouse! Park rangers in neat outfits! Multimedia histories! A museum. The church would make a fucking great museum. And reenactments! Goddamn, reenactments. People dressed up like French soldiers and people dressed up like the ol' Caribs. The French people could chase the Carib people to the edge of the cliff and they could act like they're jumping off! Hell, man, people would love that!"

I slip through a rusted chain-link gate and step around and between grave markers, the names worn down, some rubbed completely away by the elements—the wind, the rain, the saltwater. Leslie calls to me, hollers my name, but I ignore her. Then I hear her call to Senator. I can see Senator in her hotel room tonight and I can hear her shouting out his name, all that grief and guilt and shame, everything rushing through her body at once, his black arms holding her tight until everything has drained and she is spent and she decides that it is time for him to go home.

I follow the path toward the cliff face. The wind blows steady off the sea and I can smell the salt in the air. The sun sits low on the horizon. It's beautiful, so beautiful, that it seems impossible to imagine death here, at this very place, people throwing themselves off the cliff, one after the other, so certain of death, and still running to the cliff and then out and over and down and into—what? nothing? darkness? light? A tangled mass of bodies below, the sea washing the rocks clean of the blood and the torn muscle and the broken bone.

When I reach the end of the path, I peer over the edge to the sea below. My body wavers, my equilibrium off. I can feel the alcohol in my blood, the sun on my skin. I know I am sunburned and dehydrated, more than a little drunk. When the wind kicks off the sea, I am chilled. Beneath me, halfway down the cliff, still far above the water that crashes against the rocks, I see a white shape tangled in the brush. I squint, strain to see, to give it definition and form. I get down on my hands and knees, needing something solid beneath me, my hands on the edge of the cliff, my knees on the hard, rocky ground. I know I'm drunk, but still I lean forward. I reach out and reach down, trying to touch it, needing somehow to touch the shape beneath me, but I can't tell if I can reach it from here, my sense of perspective failing me somehow, but still I keep reaching, just a little bit further, until I realize it's only an old mattress. Someone has tossed an old twin-sized mattress over the edge, and it's caught on a narrow outcrop of rock.

Then I feel my body let go, feel it pull free of the earth. The vomit rushes up through my throat, the burn of the stomach acids, and I'm falling, I'm over the edge, everything rushing past me now, but then I feel a hand on my chest and another hand on my back, and I'm not falling, it's Senator, and he's pulling me away, pulling me back. I try to yell at him, try to tell him to let me go, to let me fall, damn it, but I can't say anything, the vomit gets in the way, and he doesn't let go, keeps his hands right there, one on my chest, one on my back, and he carries me away from the edge, back into the cemetery, where I pound my fists against his chest, just pound against his chest, just pound.

Induction Ceremony

C rawford stood in the doorway to the gymnasium that night, more beautiful than my wife. The long lines of her form, the grace of her movements, the breasts that seemed firm beneath the white blouse. She bent at the knees, set down a black leather shoulder bag, and draped a long wool coat over it. She picked up a stray basketball. It doesn't mean anything to admit this, to state it objectively: Crawford, in that moment, in black slacks and black pumps, before we knew, before we understood, was more physically attractive than Marla, love her as I do.

We were there on a windy night in late February, the gym warm and familiar. I held a ball at my hip, already breathing hard. A few of the others had stopped too and turned to the doorway. Maybe it was the basketball in her hands, the way she gripped it. Maybe it was the way she cocked her head sideways and then squared her shoulders to the basket. Maybe it was the heavy makeup, the thick musculature of the neck, a recognition of the eyes. Then we were looking at each other, holding our breaths, looking over our shoulders.

"Crawford?" Nichols said. "Crawford?" he said again.

She put the ball on the floor, took a pair of hard dribbles with her right hand, then crossed over to her left, leather slapping wood.

"Who else?" she asked.

The voice was indeed Crawford's, somehow, yet it was not. Higher now, undoubtedly affected by the estrogen treatments and her own conscious affectation. I suspected that she had worked hard at this, harder even than Crawford had worked those summers when we would come to the gym every morning at six to scrimmage and lift weights, make ourselves bigger, stronger, faster.

No one moved. We were too stunned to do anything but stare, to try to decide for ourselves if it was real, if this was Crawford in women's clothing or Crawford in a woman's body. If this was Crawford.

She tossed her head back and laughed and flipped the ball toward the basket—it fell short—then ran her hand through her long auburn hair, the beautiful girl who'd caught all the boys staring at her and was enjoying every moment of it.

How long had it been since we'd assembled like this? All those hours we'd spent here in our youth. The wind sprints, the lay-up drills, the chest passes, the jump ropes, the three-man weaves. Coach's voice—*Fill the lane! Fill the lane!* And the games. Those packed houses on Friday nights, the cheerleaders in their short skirts, the cake raffles, the pep band. How loud the trumpets sounded in the gymnasium, the brass echoing off the cement block walls. Our parents, red-eyed from work; our classmates, sneaking peppermint schnapps in the parking lot; and our girlfriends—those small bodies, those slender hips, all those promises yet to be fulfilled. Twenty years and we still knew where all the dead spots in the floor were found.

Finally she said, "I'm going to change." She collected her shoulder bag and her coat and walked across the gymnasium toward the doorway to the girls' locker room, the heels of her pumps clicking on the wooden floorboards.

"Girls' locker room is locked," Griffin said.

"I'll use the boys'," Crawford replied, not breaking stride. "Nothing I haven't seen before."

We are one of those small, rural Midwestern communities that fills the gaps in the landscape, filled with little but modest hopes and modest failures. The railroad tracks were torn apart long ago, and now the interstates and freeways to the north and to the east channel business and people elsewhere. In the winter, the corn and alfalfa fields lie quiet beneath a thin layer of snow and ice, and fishing shanties darken the gray surface of the frozen lakes. Inside Colters and Vanguard, men and women sand the rough metal edges of mufflers and tailpipes or screw hinges on side panels of camper trailers. At night, we gather in the high school, to attend band concerts, to play bingo, to debate the sex education curriculum, to watch basketball. Every time we go in, we are greeted by the trophies, the cut nets, the yellowed news clippings and the time-softened leather Spalding with every player's signature. A sheet of white paper lists the typewritten scores in chronological order, one by one. And in the middle of it all, there is a black-and-white photograph of Crawford, frozen in mid-air, his body stretched long and graceful, the ball maybe a foot or two away from his fingertips, his release just completed, an opponent sealed to the ground beneath him, staring hopelessly upward. In the picture, Crawford is young, beautiful, smooth, perfect.

After graduation, Crawford had gone west to college, a school like Stanford or Berkeley, no one really seems to recall. The West was so far away from here, and he'd returned rarely in the first few years, usually at Christmas to see his folks. And then not at all. Most of us remained. Some went away and returned. Traxler took over his father's farm and was elected to the village council. Nichols coaches the junior varsity baseball team and Boyle runs a bait-and-tackle shop. Every March, on the eve of the state tournament, three or four of us gather in the locker room to give an inspirational speech to the next team. Always it ends the same—with Crawford and that shot in the photograph, the ball arcing through the air as time expires and the buzzer sounds and the crowd holds its breath. Then everything exploding as the ball drops through the net and we win the game and the state championship. It's still the best moment of our lives.

The basketball we played that night bore little resemblance to the game we'd played as youths. None of us still played on a regular basis and, after an overzealous beginning—I came ready to full-court press, squatting down and slapping the floor with the palms of my hands—the game deteriorated into an unending series of misfires, bricks, errant passes, traveling violations, and time outs. We walked the ball slowly up the court with each change of possession, breathing too heavily to speak, threw the ball around stagnant zone defenses, one or two defenders making half-hearted attempts to cut off the passing lanes, then we fired up wild shots from wherever we stood.

No one knew how to handle Crawford, her hair pulled into a ponytail, her blue nylon shorts only partially covering her smooth, bare legs. Boyle, always our best defender, undersized but aggressive, started off guarding her man-to-man—man-to-woman—but anyone watching would've had a difficult time recognizing Boyle's assignment, given how far he remained from her. When we switched to a zone defense, the pattern continued for the rest of us. We gave her plenty of space, let her drive to the basket if she wished, let her post up if that was her plan. None of us wanted to touch her. None of us wanted to know how real the change was. As teammates, we had spent many hours pounding our bodies against one another, hips against hips, arms entangled, elbows, knees, hands. Hands everywhere. And in the summer, we'd allowed a few girls to join our games and we'd shown them no special favors, hand-checks on the hips, hard fouls under the hoop.

For her part, Crawford didn't play like a girl. I could not explain the science of the operations she'd undergone or the changes the hormonal treatments had wrought on her body, and it wouldn't be accurate to say she still moved like she had then, because she didn't; the physiology was all different, the hips, the breasts, the butt. She labored like the rest of us, dogged by age; she still had a tendency not to follow her shot; and she didn't move left as well as she did right. But there were moments, brief flashes of an almost ghostly nature that reminded us that this was Crawford and if it was that Saturday afternoon all over again and if we were trailing by one and the clock was racing toward zero, she would still be the one to take the shot and she'd still come through for us as she did then. Without hesitation. Just the ball in the hands and then in the air and then in the bottom of the net.

So we played, hanging on, gulping for breath, leaning over and tugging downward on our shorts every chance we had. We didn't play long. Though some of us had been anticipating this night more than the induction ceremony to follow the next evening—the chance to be back on the court, to bank a shot off the glass backboard, to make the perfectly timed bounce pass—the excitement quickly dissipated, our lungs empty, our muscles burning, our joints aching. Soon we were all pulling on our sweats and packing our bags for the drive to Curly's.

Griffin rode with me. So did Traxler, his long legs pulled up to his chest in the back seat of my Honda Civic. As soon as the doors closed, I waited for Griffin to let loose, but he didn't. Everything had been Griffin's idea—the new athletic hall of fame, the induction ceremony on Friday night, the decision to begin with us, to induct us as a group—the 1981 Class D state championship team. He was an assistant coach now and thought it would provide incentive for the current team, a team of high expectations, a team that had done real well all year. Some thought it might be the best team since us, maybe the best ever. Griffin wanted to let them see what the future could hold for them—a plaque in the hallway, a perennial place in the Fourth of July parade, unceasing honor and praise.

I started the engine and turned the heater on full blast and let the car run for a few minutes, allowing the wiper blades to brush away the layer of fresh powder. Then I eased the car through several inches of newly fallen snow in the unplowed parking lot. Griffin sat with his arms crossed against the cold. No one said a word until Traxler said, "You just ran a stop sign," and we all shook our heads, staring straight ahead into the night, a million snowflakes lit up by the headlights.

When we arrived at the bar, we pulled several adjacent tables together and draped our coats over the backs of our chairs, and asked Dan Sanders, whose family had owned the bar for three generations now, to start a tab, bring pitchers of everything and some nachos and a couple of pizzas with lots of meat. Crawford excused herself to use the women's restroom. "Need to freshen up," she said. As soon as she was gone, Traxler wanted to know if she could do it.

"Do what?"

"You know."

He pumped one fist against the palm of the other and we laughed like junior high boys and whispered, "Shhhhh." But, of course, we all wondered the same thing.

"Do you think he's done it?" Traxler asked.

"I don't think it's just cosmetic," Rivers said.

Then Boyle said, "If my Ryan ever came to me and said, 'Dad, I want to be a girl,' I'd smack him 'til his face fell off."

When Crawford emerged from the hallway near the restrooms, she had washed her boyish face and reapplied a fresh layer of makeup and her hair had been brushed and fixed, still pulled back in a ponytail, wrapped with a blue scrunchy. As she walked across the room, I wondered what it felt like to be Crawford, what it felt like to be a woman, to feel your body encased in all that smooth skin, the downward pull of breasts, not to have a penis dangling between your legs.

At the table, Boyle tried to lure her into the history of her life, the twenty years we'd lost. She deftly dodged, providing only brief answers—her house (a bungalow not far from the Santa Monica Pier), her work (vice president at a bank), her cat (a vicious female Siamese that a friend had given to her before he died). She avoided everything we truly wanted to know, as in control here as she was in the gymnasium, still moving confidently, even without the ball, slipping between the gaps.

I tried to pretend that I was not watching every move—the way she handled the pitcher of beer, the way she lifted the glass, how she drank, how she sat back in her chair and crossed one leg over the other—the way women do, like scissors, not like men avoiding emasculation. She folded her hands in her lap, her nails painted red, her gaze drifting to the front of the bar, to the window and the snow outside. What did she see? Did she see what we could not see? Had the change—from man to woman— given her a second sight? Had it revealed to her a world yet dark to us? I wanted to ask her the secrets.

When I had the chance, I asked her about Los Angeles and the coast and she told me about surfing and ethnic cuisine and herbal supplements. I said, "I've never been there—California—but I've always wanted to go, never been anywhere really."

Crawford nodded toward my hand and I looked down and realized I'd been fiddling with my wedding band, a habit, twisting it around my finger.

"Marla," I said. "Marla Langway. Three kids."

"Really?" Crawford said. "No shit? I never would've guessed. Good for you."

I smiled, the way you smile when you realize yours is the consolation prize. She asked, so I told her about Marla and the children and the house on Elm and teaching at the high school. "Fifteenth year now, same ol', same ol'." Then Nichols said, "Damn, you two talk like a pair of old girl-friends." I made a face at Nichols and flipped him the bird. Crawford just leaned back in her seat and took a drag on her cigarette. She blew a narrow stream of white smoke into the air.

"When did you know?" Traxler asked.

"Know what?" Crawford said.

"That you . . . I don't know."

"Know that I was a woman?"

"Yeah. Sure."

"I always knew."

"Do you sleep with men?" Boyle asked.

"I don't think that's any of our business," Rivers said.

"Yes," Crawford said.

"Yes? You sleep with men."

"Yes."

We drank our beer. I had more questions that went unasked: basket-ball camps and shared bedrooms, the girls she'd dated in high school and what had happened when she had been alone with them; what she had thought when she was alone with us, if she'd ever wanted to sleep with one of us, if she would want to sleep with one of us now. I wondered if she had any diseases, like AIDS. The more I drank, the cruder my thoughts became. Did she have a vagina? Did she take it up the ass? What did she sound like when she came? I wondered what it would be like to touch her, to pass my fingers over her skin. How would it feel?

When the conversation turned to the present team, we admitted that we had mixed emotions—proud alumni, jealous ex-stars, true blue fans of the Magi. Finally Porter said, "I hope they lose—not tomorrow night. Fuck tomorrow night, a league title, no big deal. Anyone can win a league title."

"They're not as good as we were," said Seabaugh, Seabaugh who rode the bench the entire season.

"We could still beat 'em."

"No inside game."

"We had no weaknesses."

"None."

"Whatsoever."

And then we were laughing again, a bunch of middle-aged men jealous of their unrivaled position within the community. "Like a bunch of ugly-ass old women," Nichols said, "worried the pretty young things are gonna' steal our men." Nichols stood and began to pirouette, bending his wrist and speaking with a lisp, as effeminate as a 250-pound farm boy can be. "Am I pretty? Tell me I'm still pretty. Tell me you still like my tight ass." He bent over and wiggled it toward us. We cowered in horror, screamed, waved him away, and told him to sit down.

Boyle turned to Crawford. "That's funny, don't you think? I sure think so."

He kept baiting her, trying to get under her skin. But Crawford only gave him a tight smile of dismissal, and I wondered what it was that allowed her to do this, some quality she seemed to have acquired, which all beautiful women seem to possess, this ability to blow off men like Boyle. Did she pick it up somehow with the hormone treatments, the surgeries? A certain bitchiness.

We complained about the most recent property tax assessments and the sharp decline in orders at Colters, and soon we lamented the problems with the dam and then Rivers rescued us with tales of his recent trip to Vegas. We agreed our lives had changed, so much had changed, and yet it was good to be back together, everyone here, glad everyone could make it, some things never change. But then we looked around the table and saw Crawford. There was a nervous chuckle and a clearing of throats.

Dan delivered a fresh set of pitchers and we ordered more nachos and a few people lit cigarettes, shrugging their shoulders. And then Boyle sat back in his chair and said, "What is this about anyway, Crawford? You coming back like this. Now. Because we don't need this shit, you know. This isn't Hollywood."

The jukebox was still playing and there were other conversations around our tables and conversations in other parts of the bar and darts thumped against the south wall and Dan had the dishwasher running, but no one around our tables heard anything else, only heard Boyle's voice cutting through it all.

We all turned to Crawford. There was perspiration on her upper lip and I could see the black roots of her hair and the crow's feet around the eyes and her chest rising and falling. She held her hands beneath the table and I knew they were shaking.

"Let it go already," I said. "We're all adults here."

"Crawford always was your little boy," Boyle said.

"What do you mean by that?"

"I don't think I need to explain."

Rivers said to Crawford, "They'll laugh at you, call you names. We're just trying to protect you."

"Yeah," said Griffin. "You know how it is here."

Crawford's gaze moved slowly round the tables, taking us in one by one, but she didn't say anything. We fidgeted with our napkins and beer mugs and plates and shifted in our seats. We all knew how it was here, how it had been. How it had always been. We were the 1981 Class D state champions.

Crawford was the first to leave. She seemed to know that all we wanted to talk about was her and we couldn't do it while she was with us. She pushed back from the table and made her apologies. She explained she was weary from the day's journey—the flight from LA, the drive from Detroit Metro, the basketball—"so winded," she said, and then the beer. She admitted she didn't drink much beer anymore; most often it's just a glass of wine or a martini to unwind on an evening. From her purse, she dropped a ten-dollar bill onto the table and said she'd see us tomorrow— "Big night! Woo-hoo!" she said. We half-heartedly lifted our glasses in a mock toast, everything tumbling like a loose ball out of bounds and into the street and into the path of an oncoming car. She made a wide berth of the table and pulled her coat close as she pushed open the door. We watched out the front window, but she turned left.

As soon as the door closed, Boyle said, "Fuck it. I'm not gonna be there if he's gonna be there. No fucking way. I don't need this."

Rivers spun a bottle cap on the table. "We can't back out now," he said. "Everybody's coming. My parents. My kids. We can't not show up."

"Who's going to explain?" Seabaugh asked.

"Who needs to explain?" said Boyle. "Let Crawford."

"They'll crucify him," Rivers said. "It'll be brutal."

We nodded again.

"So what do we do?" Griffin asked. "I don't want the boys to see this. Not before the fucking game."

"We're a team," Nichols said. "We've always been a team. We stick together through thick and thin. That's why we won it all, remember?"

When I arrived home, I found Marla on the couch in the living room, already in pajamas, her feet tucked beneath her. The light from the floor lamp angled over her shoulder and illuminated the novel she was reading. Everything had been cleaned and put away, the dishes from dinner washed and the table cleared. My students' quizzes were in a single pile on my desk and the kids were in bed. I set down my gym bag and she glanced upward.

"You look tired," she said.

I nodded. She removed her glasses and set them atop the book.

"You okay?" she asked.

I nodded again. "Yeah. Tired, that's all. Sore."

I sat beside her on the couch and unlaced my high tops. I told her about Crawford and the sex-change operation and the reaction of the guys; playing basketball against her, the trip to the bar, everything Boyle said. I told her there had been some discussion after Crawford left about the ceremonies the following night. I loosened the drawstring on my sweatpants and slid them off and then peeled down the rubber sleeve brace I wore on my left knee.

"What was he like? When you dated him?" I asked.

"Why?"

"Curious, that's all."

"I don't know. That was a long time ago."

"Are you surprised?"

"About what? The sex change? Of course. Why wouldn't I be? Twenty years. Geesh."

"Did you ever wonder?" I asked.

"About Crawford?"

"Yes."

Marla pulled her robe tight against her body.

"I was sixteen," she said. "I wondered many things. If he liked what I wore, if he liked what I smelled like, if he thought of me during games, if his father would ever quit drinking, if he preferred my hair up or down, if he thought I was ugly with my glasses on."

"But you didn't wonder . . ."

"If he was going to undergo a sex-change operation? No. I didn't even know you could do that, I don't think."

Marla placed her book on the coffee table and stood. It was late. We both needed to be up early in the morning to get ourselves ready before packing the kids off to school.

"He said he always knew he was a woman," I said.

Marla shrugged. "Maybe it just took him awhile to sort things out."

I nodded. I wanted to ask more questions, but I was afraid that if I started they wouldn't stop. Or maybe I was just afraid of the answers. Marla told me she was going to bed and I nodded and said I would join her soon, after a shower.

Before she disappeared up the stairs, she turned to me and said, "It was never serious between us."

In bed I couldn't sleep. I was physically exhausted, my muscles cramped. Marla lay on the far edge of the bed and I leaned toward her, unwilling to let her get too far from me.

"Did you sleep with him?" I asked.

Marla didn't answer. She kept her back to me, but I knew she had heard me.

"Not that it matters now," I said.

Marla rolled onto her back and turned her head to look at me. "Why do you want to know?" she asked.

"I think a husband should know these things."

"You've never asked before—about any of my ex-boyfriends."

I shrugged. "Aren't all brides virgins?" I said, trying to be funny.

"We've been married for sixteen years," she said. "Does it matter?"

I wanted to say it didn't, but suddenly it did. I wanted to know everything. I wanted to know why she was being so evasive. I wanted her to answer now, before she could construct a well-crafted lie.

"You did, didn't you?"

Marla turned away from me and instinctively I reached out and placed my hand on her waist, in the curve between her breasts and hips. "I'm not going to deal with this ridiculousness," she said. "It's too late. Now go to sleep."

For the next hour, I lay awake in bed and stared at the ceiling. I envisioned Crawford and Marla in the back seat of his father's Oldsmobile, in her bedroom on the second floor of her parents' house, in the back row of the movie theater in Sturgis. I had a difficult time remembering what Crawford looked like then, could only see her as the boy in the photograph, the basketball uniform and the shot, or as the woman who had strolled into the gymnasium a few hours before. I imagined Crawford and Marla naked and I wondered what Crawford looked like naked now, if there were scars, cruel red lines across her body. I wondered how she explained it to a man the first time she undressed for him.

At three in the morning, Marla awakened and realized that I was not sleeping. I told her it was just my muscles and joints, everything sore. She offered to make me a warm glass of milk. I felt her bare foot on the inside of my calf.

"It's so weird," I said.

"What is?" she whispered.

"I keep thinking about all those times in the locker room, you know. And about Boyle and Crawford."

"What about Boyle and Crawford?"

"You know. The rumor."

"What rumor?" she asked.

"You don't remember? Geez, it must have been sixth or seventh grade. A few of the guys were spending the night together, maybe at Boyle's, a 3-on-3 tournament the next morning or something. And they started comparing peckers, who was bigger than who, that sort of thing, the sort of thing you do when you're in sixth grade. And Boyle got turned on and got hard and Crawford grabbed his pecker and Boyle came all over the place."

Marla ran her hand across my bare chest. "You sure you don't want a glass of milk?"

"Nah, I'm good. We just thought it was funny at the time. We didn't think anything of it."

"I remember now," she said.

"You do?"

"Yes. I was in the hallway outside the bandroom when I heard. But . . ."

"Go on."

"But the way I heard it, it wasn't Boyle," she said.

"It wasn't? Then who was it? Rivers?"

"It was you," she said.

"Me?"

"Yes. In the rumor. I was in the hallway outside the band room when I heard."

I tried to remember Boyle's bedroom. The upstairs hallway. The half-bathroom to which Boyle—Rivers?—had fled in embarrassment. Had I even been there that night? Who had told me?

"Why do you think this?" I asked.

"Everyone knew."

"It was just a mean rumor," I said. "You know how those things go. Stories boys make up."

Marla nuzzled her face into my neck. "Go to sleep," she said.

"Have we talked about this before?" I asked.

She shook her head.

"Why not?" I asked.

"I don't know. It's not important."

"You're right. It isn't. It was a long time ago."

"Yes."

"I'm not gay," I said. "I've never been gay."

"I know, Todd."

She kissed me on the cheek.

"It wasn't me. I think it was Porter."

In the darkness of our bedroom, I tried to remember the season. Was Nichols right? Had we stuck together through thick and thin? Is that why we won it all? In a three-week stretch in March, we won seven in a row, the only seven that really count if you want to be remembered forever. But we lost the last three games of the regular season—Coach was bitterly silent at Senior Night—and we barely won half our games from December through February. Nichols and Rivers were suspended for three games when they were caught drinking vodka in the FFA room after practice. Porter pounded the crap out of Seabaugh when he found Seabaugh in the backseat of his car with his hand down the pants of Sherry Blackwood, Porter's girlfriend, the one who refused to even let him touch her bare breasts.

And Crawford? At the Christmas tournament in Bronson, Coach nearly kicked him off the team because he pulled the elastic from his socks and allowed them to slump around his ankles. "It looks sloppy! It looks juvenile! We all wear them to the knees!" Later, he ripped the little gold stud from Crawford's ear and it bled for three days. Did we rally around Crawford? Who defended him in front of Coach? Did anyone? Sometime in January Crawford began to paint his fingernails, a new color every week, until the tournament in March when he painted them black and then stuck with black—we insisted that he stick with black. We were winning, and we were all superstitious now. And then there was that afternoon when Boyle stood in the middle of the locker room and accused Crawford of staring at everybody's dicks.

"You homo."

Crawford turned to face the inside of his locker. He held the towel loosely around his waist, but everyone could see the small tent it formed—he had a hard-on. He stared into the box of his locker and we watched his shoulders rise and fall as he tried to breathe deep, tried to gain control of his breathing, prayed the tent would collapse.

The next night, at Mendon, Boyle refused to pass the ball to Crawford and Crawford refused to pass the ball to Boyle until Coach finally called a time-out and hollered, "He was wide-open under the goddamn basket! What the hell is going on here? What the fuckin' hell is going on here?" The gym grew quiet, real quiet ("What did he say? Did he say the f-word?"). No one was going to say, not here, not now, "Boyle thinks Crawford is a fag." So Coach yanked Boyle and Crawford from the game and sent them to the end of the bench where they sat in silence side-by-side for the next three quarters and we lost by twenty.

It was Boyle, wasn't it?

Marla opened her eyes and closed them and opened them again.

"Have you ever wondered what it would be like to be with a woman?" I asked.

She rolled over onto her side.

"I'm going to pretend I didn't hear that," she said. "I'm going to pretend you're talking in your sleep and it's all nonsense. I'm going to pretend you're drunk."

I rose from bed and dressed. Outside, I shoveled the snow from the driveway, lifting and tossing and pushing, the metal edge of the shovel scraping against the cement of the drive until my back was sore and my hamstrings ached and I was sweating beneath my coat and the inside lining of my gloves was soaked. The night had turned clear and my breath crystallized the air around me. The ball didn't bounce well in the cold, the rubber dull and heavy, the cover worn smooth by years of pickup games.

I was the one who was supposed to take the shot. That's the way Coach drew it up in the chaos of the huddle, our final timeout, six seconds to go, his voice hoarse, screaming over the bands and the crowd and all those years of disappointment. This was his best team ever, he'd finally show them all. And then everything went wrong. Crawford fumbled the in-bounds pass and there was a mad scramble for the ball and there were bodies everywhere. I stood in the far corner, feet frozen to the court, just waiting, and then Crawford regained control of the ball, but everyone was in the wrong place now, the timing was off, the picks and the rotation, and so the ball went to Boyle and then back to Crawford and still I just stood there and watched it all unfold before me. And then the buzzer sounded and the ball was in the net and everyone was piling atop Crawford. I felt a hand on my shoulder and I turned and someone embraced me. It was Marla. She kissed me—our first kiss—and I said, "I was supposed to take the shot."

It was me, wasn't it?

Behind me I heard the sound of tires on the snow and ice-slickened road. I turned to find a pair of headlights approach our house, slow, and then drift past. I knew the driver must be staring at me, wondering what the hell I was doing shooting baskets at four in the morning in the dead of winter. The car braked to a stop at the intersection and idled there, a cloud of exhaust billowing up behind it. The windshield was too fogged up to see the driver, but then I realized that it was Crawford. I just knew. The car sat there, waiting, as though it was waiting for me to wave or shoot so that it could proceed. But I held my ground, fingers numb, the cover of the ball wet and slick, my breathing heavy.

Finally I hollered, "Crawford, is that you?"

The driver's side window began to lower and I stepped forward in the drive, trying to see more clearly. As I approached the edge of the street, the driver leaned toward the open window, and in the yellow of the streetlight, I saw a woman's face and I looked hard. I wanted to see something I could recognize.

"Crawford, is that you?" I repeated, more quietly this time.

"Yeah," she said. "It's me."

"I thought I recognized you," I said. I held the ball in front of me with both hands. "All these years. People change. You can barely recognize yourself."

She nodded. I waited for her to speak, maybe to explain, though explain what, I didn't know.

"What are you doing out here?" Crawford asked, her voice dry and masculine.

"I was about to ask you the same thing," I said. "Couldn't sleep."

"They have pills for that, you know, little blue pills."

She held her hand up as though she was pinching a pill between her thumb and forefinger. I smiled. "Can I ask you something?"

"Sure," Crawford said.

"Did anything ever happen between us?"

"Anything? Like?"

I opened my mouth but said nothing, uncertain of how to phrase it.

"Oh, you mean . . ." She nodded.

"Because," I said, "see, I have this memory . . ."

She held her hand palm open to stop me. "We were drunk."

"We were in the sixth grade."

"It just happened."

"But did I want it to happen?"

"It's nothing to be ashamed of."

I rolled my eyes. "You've never been ashamed of anything," I said. "That's the difference between you and me. You don't know the meaning of the word 'ashamed.'"

Maybe I was trying to be light, funny, even I couldn't tell. But she glared at me, hard.

"No," she said. "I've always been ashamed of everything."

I tried to recover, to bring things back to . . . to what? Twenty years, all those dead spots. "I didn't mean anything," I said.

"It's late," she said.

I nodded. "Yes. It is."

She leaned back into the car, into the shadows. The window rose and she disappeared behind the streaked condensation of the windshield. The car moved forward and turned right and I followed the red taillights until they disappeared behind the neighbors' houses.

Friday night arrived cold and clear, filled with bright, icy stars. The school parking lot overflowed with cars and trucks and they were parked end-to-end up and down the surrounding streets. Faces were painted. Banners covered every available space on the gymnasium walls.

A half-hour before the varsity game was scheduled to begin, we assembled in the library—the 1981 Class D state championship team, our wives and our girlfriends, our children and those parents who were still around, still alive, still as proud now as they had been then. The athletic director and the superintendent of schools and the mayor were there. We stood around and ate cake and drank punch and made small talk. The athletic director went over the plan for the evening, how the ceremony was going to go. He took attendance and only paused briefly when Crawford acknowledged her presence—Nichols had tipped him off, just so there would be no surprises.

Late in the fourth quarter of the junior varsity game, we began to make our way toward the gymnasium, squeezing our way through the overflow crowd that tumbled into the hallway. We lingered near the entrance to the gymnasium and when the final buzzer sounded, someone said, "Overtime," and our hearts beat that much faster, the delirium in the gymnasium already building to a fever pitch. "Insane," Rivers said, and there were smiles all around.

We shifted back and forth on our feet. We greeted old friends and shook hands and exchanged hugs and accepted slaps on the back. Everyone had a favorite memory of the season or a favorite story from high school. We introduced our wives to people they'd never met and we were the center of attention again, everyone pushing up to shake our hands and touch our arms as though some magic still remained. In the fluorescent light of the crowded hallway, we tried not to look each other in the eyes, fearful of what we would see there: our own aging bodies reflected back to us. Our wives told us all our friends looked so much older, but we knew the truth.

Crawford stood off alone, unrecognized. She wore a sharp blue dress, quite tasteful, and we had to admit she carried it off well. Her auburn hair fell to her shoulders in soft curls and with the attention she'd given to her makeup—to the eye shadow and the lipstick and the blush—it seemed impossible to tell. She looked as though she'd been a woman from the moment of her birth and she could pass for twenty-five. Teenage boys in blue jeans and letter jackets, cowboy boots and painted faces, all paused to give her a long, lingering second glance. For her part, Crawford seemed unruffled, unfazed. Like she always had.

I still wondered why she had come and as she stood apart from us— apart from everyone—I watched her with a mixture of disdain and jealousy and love. Yes, love. How could I not? I could still see her body as it had been—the body of that teenage boy, the ball just released from his hand, and what could I begrudge her? She would be gone the following day. She wouldn't stay. I didn't even need to ask.

When the junior varsity game finally ended, the buzzer sounding yet again, the athletic director shouted instructions for us to get in line. As soon as the players were off the court, the gymnasium went dark and a spotlight fluttered over to the doorway. Over the familiar, muffled strains of the fight song and the rising thrum of the crowd, "Radioman" Dawson began to introduce us, one-by-one, calling us by our old nicknames, reminding the packed house of the achievements of our youth. As our names were called, we each stepped into the spotlight and strode across the floor, and when we arrived at center court, we stood on the block C, and we exchanged high-fives and hugs and pumped our fists in the air, the adrenaline pumping through our bodies in time with the beat of the bass drums. We tried to act dignified, like adults, but then Nichols did a little dance and even Boyle threw kisses to the crowd, so that by the time Dawson reached the last of us—Crawford, who else could it be?—and over the P.A. system came Dawson's crackling, audiotaped radio call—"Crawford on the wing with two to go . . . he's got to take the shot . . . he's got to take the shot . . . it's . . . Yes! Yes! We win! We win!"—the entire crowd was on its feet and going nuts, the vision still crisp and clear of that boy's body and that last shot.

Then through the double-doors at the south end—where we had first seen her the night before—Crawford stepped into the gymnasium and into the harsh brightness of the spotlight. She strode toward us with confidence, her high heels clicking on the polished wooden floor, the hem of her dress sashaying around her, her right arm extended in a beauty-queen wave, a huge grin on her face. She moved as though the court belonged to her and to her alone, as though the moment belonged to her, and we knew—every one of us, standing there in the darkness of center court with our arthritic knees and our thick bodies and our divorces and our modest jobs and our twenty years of modest misfortunes—that it did, it always had. When the gymnasium fell silent, first in confusion and then in recognition, we waited for the catcalls and the whistles and the crude names and maybe they came and maybe they didn't, but in the darkness, we kept clapping—I kept clapping—just the palm of one hand against the palm of the other, until the house lights came up and the pep band kicked in and through the locker room door burst a dozen teenage boys, whooping, hollering, dreaming of the best moment of their lives.

Punnett's Squares

We arrived in twos and threes in second-hand cars and rusted and mud-stained pickup trucks. In the crisp morning dawn we gave our names to the crew leader, who misspelled them on his clipboard, and then we stood around the edge of the cornfield in limp-shouldered clumps. Cocooned in cotton sweatshirts and yellow and blue rain slickers, or black trash bags with a hole cut out for the neck, we milled about in the rutted dirt and the stinkweed and the tall grasses, not yet awake. The ten-hour day would begin cold and wet and would end beneath brutal summer sun, our bodies dry and red, our hands callused and raw. But for the moment, we kicked mindlessly at half-buried rocks with the toes of our water-logged canvas tennis shoes, fingerless brown garden gloves stuffed into the back pockets of our cut-off denim shorts. The crew leader, one of the Stauffers back from college for the summer, asked if there were any new bodies. Two hands were raised. He called them over and took hold of a stalk of seed corn and demonstrated the proper technique for removing the tassel: thumb down, lift straight up.

Tommy leaned toward me. "Two words," he said. "Corn sex."

I laughed and people turned to stare at us. Tommy looked back over his shoulder as though the laughter had been tossed from somewhere deep behind us.

Another car swung into the dirt drive and three Amish teenagers piled out along with the crew chief's daughter, a fifteen-year-old with a driver's permit and an oversized sense of authority. Her aunt, a woman in her forties, a widow, her gray socks slumped around her legs, red and inflamed from mosquito bites and corn rash, hoisted an orange water jug from the back of her pickup, and set it on the ground. The Amish girls stood together, apart from the rest of us, in their long skirts, plain and solid, white bonnets, black stockings, and heavy black shoes, mystery upon mystery. One of the Yoder boys snapped off a tassel, hard, like a neck, and when the crew leader looked the other way, whipped it at his brother who turned, the tassel glancing harmlessly off the hip.

"Quit looking for her," Tommy said. "She isn't here."

"I'm not," I lied.

"It ain't never gonna happen."

"I didn't say I wanted it to."

"We all want it to."

"Not me."

"Good. That's the proper attitude to take."

The crew leader checked his watch and started to assign people to blocks and rows. Tommy and I fell in together wordlessly, side-by-side, taking two female rows adjacent to two male rows, the first stalks in the male rows marked with swatches of metallic silver paint on the leaves. These rows would remain untouched.

Alex Berenson slumped to the row beside Tommy and stuttered out a "G-g-g-ood morning." Tommy rolled his eyes at me, but then he turned and said, "Hey," like he meant it. We were joined by one of the Turley boys from Mendon and his cousin Josh. I knew we wouldn't exchange more than two or three words with them all day. Then a boy of maybe thirteen or fourteen with a buzz cut, pink cheeks, and a pencil neck, someone I'd never seen before, came walking toward our block of six rows, his body thin and insubstantial against a backdrop of oak trees, white barns, and irrigation pipe.

"We'll be picking back on him all day," Tommy muttered.

The boy walked with his eyes downcast and never raised them as he approached, just walked directly to the far side of our block and stood there quietly beside his row. That's when I saw the left sleeve of the boy's red nylon jacket, safety-pinned to his side. Flat and empty.

The crew leader gave the go-ahead. I took one last look for her, but I could wait no longer. There was the crack and pop of dozens of tassels being pulled from the stalks, and the sullen silence of teenagers not yet awake, mechanically and quickly moving in among the wet leaves, the tassels dropping to the ground behind us, small, green missiles impacting the earth, as we began the first of maybe a dozen long, slow, half-mile walks through the field. I tried to picture Katrina Liptz—kissing lips, sucking lips, wet lips, red lips—as she had been the day before. I did not think of Sabrina Torreon or Olen Torreon—that was all yet to come. On that morning in late June, there were only rows and rows of corn, everything muffled in the damp air and the drowsiness of six A.M.

I was fifteen years old, barely 105 pounds, and the only Asian kid in a small, rural Midwestern community of well-fed, red meat and potatoes, high-cholesterol farm families of Dutch and Germanic stock. My friends called me the foreign exchange student and salespeople in the mall in Kalamazoo always spoke slowly to me. Rarely a week went by without someone asking me to teach them a bit of karate or Tai-Chi or how to eat with chopsticks. My very white, very American adoptive father referred to me as his "war prize," even though my status as an orphan had nothing to do with a war. He had brought me home with him at the end of his tour of duty with the U.S. Army in Taiwan when I was barely six months old, fulfilling a promise made one night in a bar to his best friend, a promise I'm sure my father had no inkling at the time he would have to fulfill. To my mother, unable to bear her own children, I imagined myself as a sort of consolation prize.

I reached for a tassel, guided by touch more than by sight, and I slid my hand down and wrapped my fingers around it and yanked upwards, felt the root of the tassel give way. With my opposite hand I reached for another tassel and then a third and the next and the next, the dew-soaked seeds slick on my hands. The leaves of the stalks brushed against my blue rain slicker and the soft damp earth gave way beneath my tennis shoes. The tassels were always more difficult in the morning, the stalks swollen with water, our hands cold and wet, the skin shriveled, and when I couldn't finesse the tassel, I overpowered it, bent it to my will. I ripped away the top section of the stalk. I knew I was costing the farmer yield, but he would never know.

Ahead, Tommy seemed to glide between the rows of seed corn, his body always moving forward, his hands crossing and crisscrossing above the stalks, pulling and dropping the tassels, one pulling, the other dropping, pulling and dropping, pulling and dropping. There was a steady percussion of sound, everything in rhythm. His shoulder dipped to catch an undergrown shoot, but he didn't miss a beat, caught the next tassel in stride, lifted upward, then opened his hand and the tassel fell as he reached for the next. Whenever I fell behind and the distance between us grew too great, Tommy back-picked my row until he reached me. I was always embarrassed, my thick fingers fumbling. When I muttered, "Thanks," Tommy ignored it, just walked with me up the rows until we reached the place where we had to begin again.

We hated the cornfield. This was my second season; it was Tommy's third. Still, it was better than the only other option we had—as summer help in the factories where our parents worked, bottom-rung jobs in the residue-choked air, the chemicals that stained your skin and inhabited your lungs, the relentless scream of high-speed sanders and drills, the violent rip of metal against metal. There would be the oil-slick floors to be swept again and again, and that seat across the table from your father every day at lunch or the ride home with your mother at the end of the shift.

Tommy was already pulling away from me again, pulling two tassels to every one I pulled. I didn't care. I stopped and crouched down, untied my damp shoelace and tied it again. When I stood up, I looked back for the one-armed kid, but he was nowhere to be seen. I wondered if Tommy would pick back on the kid or if he'd leave him to fend for himself. I wondered if the kid had quit and gone home, and if we'd have to go back at the end of the day to finish his rows.

"Tommy," I hollered. I couldn't see him, but I heard the rustle of leaves stop and so I knew he had heard me.

"What?" he hollered back.

I wanted to ask him about Katrina Liptz, to ask him everything he knew, but I was afraid of what he might reveal. Every morning I tried to find her in the small crowd that gathered at the edge of the field. When I found her—the long, thin girlish body; blue eyes that always awoke me from the last fits of sleep; blonde hair in a summer ponytail—I edged my way in her direction in the hope that I would somehow end up near her, perhaps in the same block, in side-by-side rows. Maybe we'd strike up a conversation, something to fill the time. We'd find something in common, make each other laugh, and realize that all this work wasn't so bad after all, not when you're amongst friends.

"Do you think she doesn't like me because I'm Asian?" I asked.

"Who?"

"Katrina."

"I don't think she knows you exist. I don't think she even knows your name."

"But even if I did?"

"Tell your name?"

"Yeah."

"Well, then I suppose you'd have to try not to act like you're acting now."

"What do you mean?"

"You're being an idiot, Ichi. If you're an idiot, it don't matter to her what else you are."

I had told Tommy I would use the detasseling money for a stereo—one of those dual-cassette portables from Sears—or put it toward a used car, if I could find one for under 500 bucks. I told him I would drive us to Sturgis, to the movies or State Line Putt-Putt Golf, but it was only Katrina I imagined with me in the car, the two of us alone. She'd wear lipstick and perfume and eyeliner. She would say yes when I asked if she wanted to park somewhere. I knew where we would go, a narrow dirt lane off Banker Street Road. I imagined her body naked in the moonlight, our secret hidden by rows and rows of corn.

By mid-afternoon, we had shed the rain slickers and the sweatshirts, and we were bare-chested beneath the white summer sun. There were long and narrow pink welts laced across my belly and my chest from the razor-edge of the corn stalks' leaves. My hands were raw and red and callused. Wrapped around my head was a rolled blue handkerchief, a makeshift sweatband. In my hand I held an aging, weathered stick, blown off an elm tree by an early spring storm. I drew its tip across the topsoil and created a box, then divided the box into smaller boxes. Inside the boxes I carved pairs of X's and Y's in various combinations.

"We've been through this before," Tommy said.

"I know, I know. But why do I have blue eyes? Tell me that, huh?"

He shrugged and raised his can of Spartan-brand cola to his lips, squinting against the sun. I swung my hand in the air to wave away gnats and retraced my topsoil script. I reminded Tommy of the relationship of dominant genes to recessive genes, of the difference between phenotypes and genotypes, of the mathematical correlations between children and parents and grandparents and great-grandparents. Since Mr. Hunter's biology class the previous spring, Gregor Mendel and Punnett's Squares had become my obsession. I had constructed hundreds of these boxes and filled them with variables for eye color and hair color, for skin tone and fullness of lips, for ear shape and nostril flare and anything else I could think of. And each time I had drawn the same spectacular conclusion: my adoptive father was my biological father.

"Why would your dad lie about something like that?" Tommy asked.

"Think about it," I said. "He's dating my mom when he leaves for overseas and promises have been made about marriage when he gets back. They haven't even had sex because they've decided to wait until marriage. They tell each other how much they love each other and promise to write every chance they get. But my dad gets to Taiwan and Mom's a long ways away, clear across the ocean, and he gets lonely and horny and . . ."

"Oh, man, do you have to say that?"

"What?"

"Horny. I don't want to think of your parents that way."

I don't laugh. I'm serious.

"This is important," I said.

Tommy set his can of pop into the dirt and stepped away from me. I watched him for a moment until I realized he was unzipping his shorts and I turned away. A moment later I heard a steady stream of urine splashing among the leaves and the topsoil, Tommy sighing deeply in relief.

"So he meets a Taiwanese woman," I said. "Who knows where, maybe in a bar, maybe on a trip into town or maybe she happens to be at the base to help with the laundry or something, maybe some sort of job. They fall in love or maybe they don't fall in love, maybe they just end up having sex because he's a good-looking guy and she's a little hottie. But she ends up pregnant and now my dad has a problem because there's my mom waiting back home. See what I'm saying?"

Tommy knew what I was saying. He'd heard me say it a dozen times in a dozen variations. I was the love-child of Bruce Lee. A descendent of royalty, the illegitimate son of Chiang Kai-shek. I was the offspring of a terrible, but passionate and brief, liaison between Chairman Mao and a secret American double-agent who had fled in disgrace to Taiwan. But those ideas were mere conjecture, fantasy. This was science.

"The woman gives birth. Me. There I am. My dad doesn't know what to do. His time in Taiwan is almost up; it's time for him to return to the States. But there is his son. There is the mother of his child. But! She dies. Gets hit by a car. Catches a stray bullet in the neck. Contracts malaria and withers away in a week. Or maybe she just decides it would be better for me to be raised in the States."

I looked at Tommy. He'd zipped up his shorts and returned to his seat. He tossed Cheetos into his mouth, his fingers coated with orange artificial coloring.

"He writes to my mother and tells her a story," I said. "Two friends. A newborn infant. A tragic car accident and the promise he had made. His time in Taiwan ends and he brings the child back with him. Adoption papers are drawn up. He kisses Mom. They hold the baby. She cries. They get married."

"You're so messed up," he said.

"Don't be such an a-hole," I said.

That's when Katrina Liptz emerged from the field, just two blocks over, and without a word we both shut up. She wore a gray T-shirt and blue running shorts and a mesh Pioneer baseball cap, her dirty blonde hair trailing behind her in one long thick braid. Her legs were nicked from the corn, and there was dried mud caked on her shoes and up her ankles, and her skin was beet-red, burned like we all were by that time of the summer, not enough sunscreen to compensate for that much sun. She walked right past us and disappeared behind the line of trees where the vehicles were parked and the lunches were stored.

"How far back you think that kid is?" I asked.

"What kid?"

"You know."

Tommy stood and wrapped his right arm behind his back and leaned over to the left, then let his head sway on his neck. He closed one eye and extended his tongue to his chin. "Thz-one?" he said, and I laughed. He ambled toward the block of corn and attempted to pluck a tassel one-handed from a row of males, struggling deliberately, wrapping his legs around the base of the stalk, then falling, dragging the entire stalk to the ground and landing hard on his ass. He moaned.

"What do you think happened?" I asked.

"To his arm?" asked Tommy. "How the hell am I supposed to know?"

He stood and dusted himself off. "Farm kids are always getting stuff sliced off. Just keep your balls away from the shredder."

I don't know if Olen Torreon grew up on a farm or if he detasseled corn when he was a teenager. My mother said that at one time he drove the ice-cream truck.

In the first week of July, Olen kidnapped his estranged and very pregnant wife, Sabrina, instigating a statewide manhunt. County police cars and unmarked FBI Fords crisscrossed the back roads of our county, searching the woods and the fields and the abandoned barns with blood-hounds and helicopters. They posted Olen's mug shot on television and in the newspaper, and spread maps and compasses across the overheated hoods of their cruisers and came away empty-handed. Rumors floated everywhere. A white Cadillac in the parking lot of a Kmart in Sturgis. Grainy images on a security camera at a gas station in Burr Oak. A goat's head amid ashes in the lot behind Olen's trailer. Olen knew the area well. Her body could rest at the bottom of a dozen lakes, in the cattails of two dozen ponds. A shallow grave, a creek bed, a dumpster, an irrigation lane, a cellar, a freezer, a crawl space, an alleyway, an attic. There are a thousand ways to dispose of a body.

Olen had just finished six months in Jackson Prison for fraud, his second stint. He found Sabrina within hours of his release. Eight months pregnant with his child and he wrestled her out of her best friend's apartment with an arm tight around her neck and dragged her body like a sack of grain down two flights of stairs. He forced her behind the wheel of her best friend's car and got in on the other side. The best friend and the neighbors who had come outside to witness the commotion stood watch as she eased the car out of the parking lot and into the road, the blue hatchback merging into traffic, turn signal flashing, then off. Then they were gone.

Every morning in July when Tommy and I drove to the cornfields and every night when we drove home again, I watched for Olen and Sabrina. I peered down two-track dirt trails that wandered back onto a farmer's property, half-expecting the convict and the pregnant woman to emerge from the corn or the trees or from behind a silo, or for a car to turn into the road, its flaps covered in mud, its lights off despite the fading light of evening. I imagined what I might do, how I would trail them, hunt them down, call the police. Better yet, I'd just take him myself, an arm around the neck, a knee to the balls. I was lifting weights six days a week for football. On those drives, the blood rushed through my veins and arteries just a little quicker, a little stronger, that surge of adrenaline.

Another set of boxes. Along the top of each column, I wrote the days of the week in crisp block letters. In the far left column, I printed a list of the stations in the weight room: bench press, inclined bench press, military press, squats, box-squats, dead lift, clean-and-jerk, lats, arm curls, leg curls, inclined sit-ups, push-ups, chin-ups. For each box, I entered the number of sets, the number of repetitions, the amount of weight where applicable. Monday: bench press, 3 sets of 15 at 150 pounds. Tuesday: box squats, 3 sets of 15–10–5 at 250 pounds. Wednesday: two-mile run in 13:56.

The weight room wasn't anything to speak of, a cement block storage room adjacent to the football field into which the athletic department had placed a Nautilus machine, two bench presses, a metal frame for squats, and a small wooden stage for clean-and-jerk. On the wall, there were posters of Lou Ferrigno and Lyle Alzado and a third that warned against the dangers of smokeless tobacco. The narrow room reeked of sweat, leather, and cold metal, and when you breathed, your lungs filled with the residue of rosin and ragweed. A paint-splattered boom box sat in the corner and pounded out AC/DC and Black Sabbath, and we grunted and yelled and screamed at each other and push-push-push-come-on-you-sissy and then the spotter eased the bar back into place and we sat up and smacked each other on the back and reminded ourselves that we had one more set.

I lifted six nights a week, taking Sunday off. "Even God rested on the seventh day," Coach Evers said. Monday, Wednesday, and Friday I worked the lower body—legs mostly—and Tuesdays, Thursdays, and Saturdays were dedicated to the upper body—arms, chest, neck, shoulders, that sort of thing. My diet was loaded with carbohydrates, proteins, milk, eggs, weight-gain powders. I was diligent, faithful, all those things you're supposed to be. All those things you have to be when you're fifteen years old, five-foot-nine, and 105 pounds. I told myself I was strong for my weight and then Charlie—a six-foot-two, 235-pound senior lineman—stepped inside the metal frame of the squat box and squatted 450 pounds five times, and in my bones I felt the crush of his body against mine when August two-a-days rolled around.

Each evening I carried a clean sheet to the weight room and filled it out as I went, then at home that night, before I collapsed into bed, I would transfer the information from that sheet into my bodybuilding journal. Through the summer, I watched the numbers grow—the sets, the reps, the weight. I calculated percentage gains, estimated future performances, stood on my mother's scales in the bathroom and weighed myself. Seated on the edge of my bed, I stripped the T-shirt from my body, flexed my right bicep, and touched it with my left hand. It was small but hard and firm. I thought of Katrina Liptz, thought of stripping off my shirt and flexing for her. I thought of the touch of her fingertips on my skin. "Here." I knew I was getting bigger, stronger. The boxes told me so.

A young woman in a hot-pink suit and white blouse stood before the front entrance of the high school, a microphone in hand. In the glare of the camera lights, the brick walls of the high school appeared fake, like a painted backdrop for a community theater play. She stated that Olen Torreon claimed that he was not the father of Sabrina Torreon's child. He'd been in Jackson Prison for six months and she was eight-and-a-half months pregnant. He said he "could do the math." Upon which the reporter revealed that in fact math had never been one of Olen's stronger subjects at Centreville High School, where administrators had with great relief granted him a diploma a decade earlier and bid him farewell.

I was stretched out on my belly across the center of the living room floor, my chin in my hands. Behind me my father relaxed in a blue La-Z-Boy recliner, his Zanzabelt softball jersey unbuttoned, his pale bare feet propped up in front of him, the toes like a row of tree stumps, the nails yellowed and brittle. My father played first base and batted fifth for the company's slow-pitch softball team, and he was basking in the afterglow of another Industrial League victory. He'd been an all-conference linebacker and third baseman in high school and still relished competition. He believed in the moral clarity of athletic achievement. Despite the stale summer air in the living room, my mother sat curled on the couch with her feet tucked underneath and a yellow afghan wrapped around her shoulders.

"I would think it would be hard to raise a child that your husband or your wife had had with someone else," I said.

My parents didn't answer. The anchorman, a man with an orange tan and lines of media authority in his face, held a hand to his earpiece and asked the woman in the pink suit for a clarification.

"Don't you think so, Dad?"

"What's that?"

"You need to get your hearing checked, dear," my mother said. "I keep telling you that. You're going deaf in that factory."

I waited for my father to answer. I wanted him to know that I knew. I wanted to blurt it all out. I wanted to tell my mother that I was my father's love child, not the offspring of two dead people from the other side of the world.

"You lift tonight?" my father asked.

"Yeah."

"Good," he said. "No pain, no gain."

"That's what Coach says."

"He gonna give you a shot at linebacker?"

I shrugged. "I don't know," I said. "I hope so."

The newscast broke to commercial. On the screen a child danced through a field of sunflowers, butterflies just beyond the reach of her small, white fingers. The voice-over extolled the virtues of a new allergy medication.

"Oh," my mother said, "I nearly forgot. Guess who I saw coming out of the bank today? The Troyers!"

"No kidding," my father said.

The Troyers were Sabrina's parents, an elderly couple who lived on a big, sweeping curve east of town.

"Sheila and I were on our way there after work—Sheila still needed to deposit her check from last week—and we were walking along past Ruth Ann's, and there they were. Everybody on the street was just gawking. Trying not to, but there they were, you know. You just couldn't help it. You felt so sorry for them."

My father shook his head. "How'd they look?"

"Old," my mother said. "I don't remember them ever looking so old."

"Losing a child like that will age you," my father said.

"They don't know if she's dead yet," I said. "She could still be alive."

For a moment, no one said anything, and I thought either my father really did need to get his hearing checked or I was again being ignored. Then he said, "She's dead. Even the Troyers understand that."

One commercial ended and another began and soon that one faded and the talking heads returned to the screen. The forecast for tomorrow was sunny and humid with a high in the mid-90s.

"A scorcher," my mother said.

Later, in my bedroom, I held a sun-faded snapshot in my hand. A man and a woman stand outside a drab olive military tent and the woman cradles an infant in her arms while the man stands with his hands in his back pockets and his standard-issue hat tipped askew. The woman wears a long dark dress, plain, but neat; her features are Asian and even in the bleached colors of the snapshot her skin appears different than his. The man is U.S. Army, young, clean-shaven, not much taller than she stands, his hair maybe blond. I always imagined it blond. They seem impossibly young to be holding their own child.

Everything I knew about Asia I'd learned from books in the library, which is to say, I didn't know much. The "Oriental" section of the two-room community library consisted primarily of histories of the Pacific Theater of Operations in World War II or coffee-table art books with a thousand illustrations of vases and bowls and cups from the Ming Dynasty in China. I would try to slip the books on Asia between books about George Washington or the Wright Brothers or baseball, lest any doubts about my loyalties be raised, and I would keep them hidden beneath my bed to be read by flashlight late at night, like pornography without the dirty pictures or dirty words.

My parents did not believe in race, and they raised me not to believe in it either. To them, I was not Asian. I was born in Asia. My biological mother was of Asian "extraction," as my father would say. These were indisputable facts of birth, biology, and geography. Of historical circumstance. But race was just the color of your skin. I was their son, an American, a Baptist and a Boy Scout, a kid from Centreville, Michigan. I had no memories of Asia, of Taiwan. So why should it matter? What did I have in common with kids from Tokyo or Seoul or Saigon? My parents raised me as the oddly colored great-grandson of immigrant farmers from Bohemia and Ireland and Amsterdam, raised me on hamburgers, goulash, and mashed potatoes, a boy who belonged to the race that used forks, knives, and spoons.

I looked at the photograph again. The man in the photo was too small, six or seven inches too small, to be the man downstairs, the man in the La-Z-Boy recliner and the Zanzabelt jersey. This was my only connection to those first six months of my life, the blank days when I lived in Asia, when I was Asian.

I thought about those boxes I'd been drawing with the grids and the chromosomes, the combinations of DNA, and I knew there was only so much I could do. Coach Evers teased me about my metabolism, how easily it burned calories, how I couldn't keep anything stored inside it seemed, and I knew he was disappointed too, had thought, "If only he had the body to match his heart." But I didn't.

When Tommy and I arrived on Saturday morning at the Buchholz field, the crew leader pulled a few of us aside and told us we were going to a different field. "A hot field," he said. We groaned and then bucked up like good soldiers. "We either get it today or we lose it and that's a hell of a lot of money for a farmer to lose."

Forty minutes later we were clear on the other side of the county. The corn we found rose well above our heads. The tassels were now thick and deeply rooted in the stalk, and Tommy and I had to stand on our tiptoes and use both hands. We would try to lift straight up with thumb down, but the stalks were too tall, and so we bent the stalk to gain leverage, but the curve of the stalk only squeezed the tassel tighter. So we would yank and yank and twist the top of the stalk and finally we would rip the stalk off well below where it should've been or the roots would break loose from the sandy soil and we would be left holding an orphaned stalk. It was both wasteful and inefficient. We moved to the next and reached up again and grabbed the tassel and pulled on it. The red pollen shook loose and fell like a burning rain shower into our eyes. We winced at the sting and closed our eyes, let the tears form. When we were well enough to open our eyes, we had to do it all over again. No one talked. It became impossible to judge the time without a watch. There was no pace, no rhythm. Soon my lower back was sore from the reach and the stretch and the twist, and we became separated in the blocks and took our breaks alone. I pissed in the irrigation ditches, only too happy to stand alone in the field with my soft dick dangling in the air. By midafternoon I considered quitting, just walking out of the field. See you next summer. But I didn't follow through. I hadn't been raised that way. So I kept plugging away alone, the red pollen lodged in my T-shirt, my socks, in the corners of my eyes. Each time I reached the end of a row, I lingered as long as possible and watched for Katrina Liptz, but then the crew leader would arrive with a fresh water tank and a paper Dixie cup and direct me to my next row.

It was almost dark when we were back-picking to get the last of the day's rows finished. Those stuck in the middle of the field nearly leapt with joy when they heard voices coming toward them, the endless row suddenly reduced to twenty tassels between them and us, now fourteen, now eight, now two, now I got the last one, good, let's go, let's get out of here, and the pleasure of walking through the field and down the row, the stalks of corn rushing by, a blur, the palms of your hands in front of you, pushing the leaves out of the way, out of your face, like a star football player rushing through a human tunnel of outstretched hands and arms. By the time I saw the trees just ahead, I wanted to run and then I did and the day was over and the sun was almost gone and we were sitting around on a Saturday night in July and wishing it would never end.

One of the Perkins twins—I think it was Matthew—said to me, "We're going to kidnap the calf."

"What calf?" I asked.

"The five-legged calf, stupid."

It was a rumor that made the rounds every spring, it seemed, but the twins insisted that this year it was true. They knew the farm and they knew the farmer and everything was hush-hush because the authorities were afraid it had something to do with PCBs in the soil or in the water and they didn't wish to unnecessarily frighten the public, to raise the fear of three-legged babies or two-headed dogs.

Tommy said he'd do it. I saw Katrina look at me. It may have been the first time all summer.

"All right," I said. "I'm in."

"Hell yeah," Tommy said. He slapped me on the upper arm and my skin burned, but I bit my tongue and held it in.

A few minutes later we were racing down County Road 87, Tommy riding the bumper of the pickup truck and laying on the horn and pulling into the passing lane, then dipping back behind the truck as we swept around a curve, the trees and the cornfields a blur to either side. Katrina sat between the twins in the truck and we hollered at the top of our lungs, the windows down, the radio cranked as loud as it could go. We overtook slower vehicles and swerved to avoid slow-moving Amish buggies. At a stop sign, the twins and Katrina and the one-armed kid jumped out of the truck and hollered, "Chinese fire drill!" and we piled out of our car and everyone ran circles around the truck and the car until a car pulled up behind us and honked its horn and then we scrambled back into our vehicles—this time Katrina came with us, tumbling into the back seat as I hurried to close the door. The twins burned rubber and rocketed through the intersection and back down the road, even faster than before.

We ended up in Nottawa at the Sand Lake Party Store. Inside there was a line of people waiting for ice cream. We hurried through the aisles for pop and chips and candy bars. We were being loud and obnoxious— the twins tossing a two-liter of Coca-Cola over the aisles—but no one cared. We emerged onto the deck in front of the store and took over a picnic table in the corner. Lights in green and red plastic lanterns were strung along the edges of the deck and the crickets were in full throat.

We spoke in hushed tones. We needed to wait for a couple hours, to make sure the farmer and his family were all in bed. There was a nearly full moon that night and so we'd be able to see okay in the darkness though there was a pair of flashlights in the truck that we could use. We devoured the pop, the chips, and the candy bars, and Tommy arm-wrestled both twins and won each time. The one-armed kid, it turned out, was a cousin of the twins. He was here for the summer with his mother who was helping out with the family fruit-and-vegetable stand over on M-66.

"What happened?" Tommy asked, nodding toward the space where the kid's second arm should've been.

For a moment, I thought the kid was going to ignore the question and I thought to myself that it was the wrong question to ask even though I wanted to know the answer as much as Tommy did.

"You get it chopped off by some piece of farm machinery?" Tommy asked. "Or do you have some sort of disease or birth defect? Were you born that way or something?"

Tommy was trying to make a joke, but he'd only made us all uncomfortable.

The kid sipped his Coke. "I cut if off myself," he said.

"You mean by accident?" Tommy asked.

"I took a hacksaw and sawed right through."

I waited for the kid to wink or laugh or for one of the twins to say, "Whatever," to slap the kid on the back and tell him, "Good one." But they were both looking down the road as though they'd heard it all before and it was all painful and true and "well, you asked." I looked to Katrina and she looked at me, the second time.

Tommy smiled. He believed he was being played for a fool.

"Come on," he said. "No way."

One of the twins said, "Time to roll," and rose to leave. Tommy held up his hand and said, "Wait. Wait."

He leaned across the table toward the kid who refused Tommy's hard gaze. Tommy seemed torn between laughter and anger, between being in on the joke and being the butt of the joke.

"Okay," Tommy said. "Why the hell would you do something like that?"

"You ask a lot of questions," Katrina said.

"So?"

"Just saying."

"Questions is okay," the kid said. "I just tell everybody the same thing anyway."

"Which is what?" I asked.

The kid turned to me as though aware of my presence for the first time.

"I tell 'em I wanted to be like my dad."

We had split into pairs and I found myself crouched over and hurrying along the edge of the cornfield, trying to keep my head down and my eyes open. The one-arm kid moved ahead of me with surprising grace and balance, while I stumbled forward, always on the edge of pitching face-first into the dirt. Silence, it goes without saying, was the operative word here as anyone knows who has ever thieved a five-legged calf. We quickly lost sight of the others, the flashlights off and pocketed, to be used only if necessary. The moon in the clear sky provided enough light to maneuver by as we slipped into the field itself to circle around the backside of the farm and approach the cattle pens from behind. Dogs were our biggest concern.

The one-arm kid led us to a wooden slat-board fence and he gripped the top board with his one hand and seemed to magically float up and over the boards, landing softly on the other side. I scrambled up behind him, grabbing the top of the boards with both hands and trying to throw my feet up and over. Instead I found my feet kicking against the boards and making a racket. The one-arm kid turned and glared at me from below. I collected myself, found a toehold and then another and with great effort pulled myself to the top. I straddled the fence, worried that it would collapse beneath me or that it would catch my balls just right and

I'd spend the rest of the night bent over in pain and bleeding through my piss-hole. Finally I swung both legs onto the other side. My foot reached in the darkness for a toehold I couldn't find and so I dropped to the ground, my hands scraping against the top board.

In a matter of seconds, Katrina, Tommy, and the twins appeared. The cattle, aware of our presence, eyed us suspiciously and began to shift themselves around the pen—not scared, just uncomfortable, nervous.

"Ever raped a cow?" one of the twins whispered to me.

"What?" I asked.

"Ever roped a cow?" he whispered this time. He winked at his brother.

The pen was large and there were maybe three dozen head of cattle spread out around a three-acre space. I tried to imagine what the five-legged calf might look like. I imagined an extra leg on a table or an appendage that rose out of the calf's back. I wondered if the calf could walk, if he tipped to one side or the other. I saw Katrina move toward a heifer and I realized there was a smaller cow behind her, a calf. Katrina waved her arm and Tommy was suddenly beside her. He scanned a flashlight over the calf, but nothing was out of the ordinary. Four legs, a tail, a head, two eyes, a nose.

I never heard the screen-door slam shut, but suddenly the farmyard was flooded with light and there were long shadows in the pen—the cattle and us and the edge of the barn and the fence and the big maple tree that rose between the farmhouse and the barn—and we were scrambling to get out of the pen, our tennis shoes slick on the wet mud. One of the twins fell and then was right back up. The cattle were frantic now, bumping up against each other, lowing and pressing back toward the corners, away from the light, away from us. There was no time for toeholds this time, I just grabbed the fence and pulled myself up and over and dropped to the ground below, landing awkwardly on my shoulder. I heard a voice in the distance, from the direction of the farmhouse. I raced to get into the cornfield, to disappear among the stalks of corn. The stalks snapped apart as we pushed through them and soon I heard only the sound of my own breathing and the rustling of the corn that I pushed aside. I cut up a row, moved quickly and easily with the grain, then pushed deeper, cutting across the rows, squeezing between stalks planted twelve inches apart. I knew I needed to orient myself to the cars and the irrigation ditch where we'd parked and the road that would lead us back to safety, but with the corn rising over my head and surrounded by the darkness, I was lost, just somewhere in the middle of the field.

I stopped and crouched down. My lungs were pounding and the muscles in my legs burned. I could feel a sliver in the palm of my right hand and I turned it upward and tried to see it in the moonlight but I couldn't. I listened for the twins or Tommy or Katrina, but I didn't hear anything. Then, a blast—it sounded like a shotgun blast—and I was on my feet and running again, back into the field, deeper, away from the farmhouse. I told myself it wasn't a shotgun blast, I wouldn't even know the sound of a shotgun blast, it was just a barn door being slammed home, the kind of thing a farmer does every night, the rusted metal of the runners requiring an extra degree of force, then sliding into place, but I didn't stop running.

Then I felt my toe catch and my body was suspended in the air, somewhere above the ground that waited in the darkness below me, and I reached out with my hands and felt the leaves of the corn passing through them and then the soil at my chin and the wind knocked from my lungs and all I could do was lie still in the dirt and concentrate on finding one breath and a second and a third.

I don't know when I realized exactly what I had tripped over. Maybe I knew even as I fell. Maybe I understood in some subconscious way while I yet lay face down in the ground, my fingers pressed beneath the topsoil. But I knew that farmers don't leave boulders in cornfields—they've all been long removed. And the stench didn't require explanation. I just knew.

She lay on her left side, her right leg draped over her left. Her right arm was extended before her while her left was pinned grotesquely beneath her, emerging behind her back. Even in the bluish light that reached down from the sky and found its way between the leaves of the cornstalks, I could see the belly ripped open, the blouse she wore pushed up, barely concealing her full breasts. Maybe I could see all that. Maybe I could see none of it. Maybe my mind filled in the blanks.

Later, they said that she had been in the field for less than 24 hours, that Olen had kept her alive, hid out in an abandoned cabin at the old Boy Scout campground until he realized she was going into labor. It was then that he panicked and drove around the backroads until he decided he couldn't delay any longer. He turned into an irrigation lane and drove back deep and parked and then forced her into the field and slit her throat and slit her belly, and when he knew she would never make it out of the field, he left her to die. It would be nearly six months before they would find him in Texas working as a security guard for a community college and taking classes in accounting. "Free tuition," he said.

I scrambled to my feet and began to run again. Vomit rose in the back of my throat, but nothing could get to the top, my windpipe still feeling closed off, until finally I had to stop and puke. I bent over, hands on my knees. As soon as I could, I started running again, wiping my arm across my lips, the sour-bitterness of vomit in my mouth. I ran toward a stand of trees that I could see above the top of the corn and it seemed like forever until I emerged from the corn and heard voices and recognized Katrina's laughter. I wanted to run to her, to embrace her, to wrap my arms around her and to protect her from what I had discovered, the awfulness of it all, but then I heard her say, "Tommy," and I stopped. There was a quality to the laughter that I knew well enough not to disturb. She said his name again. She knew his name; she would never know mine.

I held still at the edge of the field, embarrassed by the vomit on my lips, and sat down, my elbows on my knees and my hands clasped behind my head, trying to figure out what to do next. In the distance, I heard a car door slam shut and an engine start. Tommy said, "Shit," and Katrina laughed again. "Tommy," she said, "Tommy, Tommy, Tommy." I heard their footsteps pass a few rows over, the rustle of the corn, and I nearly called out for them, but I hesitated and they were gone. A few minutes later, I heard a second engine. I knew that they had decided they couldn't wait for me, that they trusted that I would find my way home, a Boy Scout after all, always prepared.

I waited in the field. I made myself wait until well past the time when the farmer would have finally decided that things were quiet for the night, that whatever it was that had spooked the cattle—a dog perhaps or maybe even a raccoon—was gone. Then the adrenaline emptied from my body and I found myself too exhausted to stand. So I waited, waited until well past the time when my parents would have shut off the lights and gone to bed, my father promising my mother to ground me for a week if not more. He would remind my mother that I was a good boy and that boys will be boys and that I had probably just gone out with Tommy and ended up at a friend's house and we were crashing there for the night. I promised myself I would leave in five minutes, it was possible just to walk back home, maybe hitch a ride, but then I waited some more, waited until well past the time that Katrina and Tommy would have eased themselves back into the front seat of his car, sweaty and exhausted and suddenly rushed to get home, past the time when Tommy would have kissed her sweetly on the cheek and given her ass one more squeeze before she closed the car door behind her and skipped across the front lawn to her house.

When I finally rose, I could see the farmhouse and the barn, nearly a half-mile distant. I walked slowly. I knew there was no need to hurry. I stayed well to the east of the area where I knew the body lay. I came around the backside of the cattle pens again and a few raised their heads as I crossed the yard. They watched me with indifference this time. Chickens hurried across my path and a cat watched me from his perch along the eaves of a tool shed. When I reached the porch, I knocked hard on the wooden frame of the screen door. I waited as long as seemed appropriate and knocked again. When the storm door finally opened, there stood a barefoot man wearing only jeans and a faded green Pioneer T-shirt. Every part of his body was thick—his forearms, his hands, his nose—and I felt like a little boy. I told him there was a dead body in his field, that I thought it was the missing pregnant woman. He ushered me inside and called 9–1–1, gave them his name and the address of the farm.

After he hung up the phone, he asked if I needed anything. "Water? Coffee?"

I shook my head.

"You okay?" he asked.

I nodded. He stood there in the middle of the living room, taking deep breaths.

"Can I ask you a question?" he said.

"Sure."

"Were you poking around the cattle pens earlier tonight, round midnight?"

"Yeah."

"What for?"

"I wanted to see the five-legged calf."

The man scratched the back of his head and then drew his hand down across his face. Even before he answered, I knew there wasn't a five-legged calf. I'd always known there wasn't a five-legged calf.

A few minutes later we walked back through the screen door and into the yard and there the farmer greeted Officer McCutcheon. Soon more officers arrived, in marked and unmarked cars. I led them into the field and to the place where I thought the body lay. This time, even before we saw the body, we smelled it, the rot of decay, and the officers swore and two or three excused themselves—to vomit, I knew—and I stood there, the corn shielding my eyes from the body, my stomach weak, but empty.

When my father arrived an hour later—after I'd given my report to the officers and received assurances from the farmer that no charges would be forthcoming against me—he looked at me with a mix of anger and relief and pride. My parents had been awake the entire night and had called Tommy's house only to be told by Tommy that he hadn't seen me. I assured my father I was fine and I tried to find a way to keep Tommy's name out of my story.

On the drive home, there was silence. The windows were down and the sun had not yet risen but already you could tell it was going to be another scorcher. I knew when we arrived home I would have to explain everything to my parents and by the time I was done I'd have to get ready for church. My father drove with one hand on the wheel and an elbow on the frame of the door. He said nothing about the body, but I knew that he was thinking of work on Monday morning when everyone would know it was his son who cracked the case, who found the missing pregnant woman. Finally, just as we reached the village limits and the wide sweeping curve that brought our small downtown into view, I asked my father why I had blue eyes.

"Genetics," he said. "Don't they teach you anything in school?"

I opened my mouth to protest, to say, "Yes, as a matter of fact, and that's why I'm asking," but then I bit my tongue. We were driving past the bank and I could picture Mr. and Mrs. Troyer there, emerging together through the plate-glass doors, each trying to support the other. I wondered if the phone call was being made or if an FBI cruiser was on its way now to the house or if the news had already arrived. So instead I asked my father if he'd ever seen a dead body.

"Yes," he said. "In Taiwan. Remember? Your father and mother."

He made the right turn onto our street, downshifting into second gear. The streetlight in front of our house flickered off. Mother waited on the front steps in her pink robe and slippers. I wanted to say, "I'm sorry," to apologize for causing them worry, for keeping them awake all night. But I said nothing. There was nothing either of us could say.

Tough Man

K ennedy was in too much pain to be embarrassed about the state of his living quarters. He mumbled a small apology, that if he had known he was going to have company, he would have made an effort to tidy up, at least to throw out the old newspapers and clean the refrigerator of its spoiled milk and moldy fruit. But she told him to hush and touched her finger to his cheek. Kennedy winced. Everything hurt, even the most gentle touch. When she disappeared into the kitchen, Kennedy leaned back on the sofa and closed his eyes. He tried to concentrate on something other than the pain. He wanted to tell her that she didn't need to stay. He wanted to thank her for her kindness. She returned with the ice wrapped in a towel and placed it against his swollen eye. Kennedy bit his tongue against the pain and reached for her hand, pushing the ice pack away. He held her hand in his hand and guided it back toward his eye, slower this time, more gently. She understood. She stroked the side of his head with her hand, his hair sweaty and sticky from the heat.

The woman told him she had always admired boxers. Her father had been a Golden Gloves district champ in Chicago. Kennedy tried to tell her he wasn't a boxer, tonight was something different, something more raw, brutal. But she wasn't listening. He wasn't even certain his sentences were coherent. He could imagine them in his mind but he was certain they weren't reaching his tongue in the same forms. She told him she thought he'd fought bravely, ferociously, and she took his hand in hers and began to peel the remaining tape from his wrists, to unwrap it from his palm. She kissed each red-raw knuckle tenderly, then rubbed each hand between hers, as though she needed to conjure it back to life, restore the flow of blood. She told him that she found men willing to step into the ring and engage in physical combat to be more attractive, more alive, that it must be some primal response on her part, an instinct, something she couldn't explain to her co-workers or her family. Kennedy pulled one hand away and touched his nose—swollen and sore—and he wondered if it would be further disfigured or just disfigured differently.

"Lean forward," she said, and he did. She grasped the bottom of his T-shirt between her fingers and lifted it up and over his head. Kennedy's chest was flushed red and damp under the lamp light. The air felt cool on his bare skin. She placed her hand on the center of his chest and leaned forward and kissed his cheek, then his ear, the sharp edge of her teeth on the lobe of his ear. She bent over Kennedy, her breasts pushing against the confinement of her little blue dress. If only I could see clearly, Kennedy thought. He wanted to taste her.

"Give me a minute," Kennedy said. He placed his hands on her bare upper arms and tried to push her back, tried to push her off him. Though he didn't want her to get the wrong impression.

"Sure," she said. "Anything you need."

She pulled herself away, modestly adjusting her little blue dress. As Kennedy rose from the sofa, he felt the room toggle from side to side, like the flight deck in a video game. He took his time to steady himself, tried to plant one foot flat on the floor, then felt her hand on his arm.

"Where are you going?" she asked.

"Bathroom," Kennedy said, or at least that's what he wanted to say and must have said because a few moments later he was closing the bathroom door behind him.

"I'll be right here," she said. "If you need me."

Kennedy couldn't figure out why he'd need her. He maneuvered himself in front of the stool and lifted the seat. He struggled to unlace the drawstring on his shorts, the white cord damp with sweat, his fingers thick and swollen. The nylon fight shorts dropped and then he lowered a pair of gray cotton shorts he wore underneath for luck. Finally he pulled down his cup and jock strap, relieved to be free of the constraint. The air felt good on his damp balls, his limp dick, as he stood there naked.

Kennedy waited for the flow to begin and after a bit of hesitation it did. But even before he saw its stream arching out and down into the toilet bowl, he knew something was wrong. Maybe it was the feeling of clot as it came through his urethra, maybe it was related to the pain in his side. The red tint of his yellow urine—blood—only confirmed it. Kennedy looked to the ceiling and swore to himself. He was trying to remember the fights, trying to remember any low blows, any kicks to the crotch or to the kidneys, but who knew? He'd taken a lot of punches, a lot of punishment. That much he knew; that much he could remember. Again he felt the room tilt, first one way and then the other. He felt the stream finish, the last few drops dribbling off the end of his dick. He shook himself off, and then reached to flush the toilet and fell into blackness.

They were all standing, on tables and chairs, clapping their hands in rhythm, a pack of coyotes. Kennedy looked across the ring to where they were gathered, and he saw Tony flapping his arms like a large bird about to take flight. His face was a burnt red, the muscles and the veins in his neck ready to pop. Kennedy bounced up and down on his tippy-toes, then bounced back and forth from his left foot to his right. He was trying to find his own rhythm, get everything coordinated—his hands, his feet, his mind. Frank was giving him instructions and the referee was giving him further instructions. Kennedy nodded, though nothing registered. Just lips moving. Words. Rose thrust both of her flabby black arms into the air and Jarred waved a sign above the crowd though Kennedy couldn't read it, didn't have time to read it. He heard the chants and knew the words less by sound than rhythm. El Presidente. El Presidente. El Presidente. It made Kennedy's heart sing.

When the bell rang, Kennedy moved to the center of the ring, and his opponent did likewise. Then in a moment that seemed surreal to Kennedy, almost untrue, something flashed in front of his face and he felt the impact flush on his nose. His head snapped back—that it didn't fall off surprised him—and he swung his arm in a wild arc in the direction from which he imagined the blow had come, and when it met nothing he swung his other arm and this time his fist struck a glancing blow.

Immediately he felt another blow to the side of his head, and so he bur-
rowed forward swinging wildly until he felt a pair of arms locked
around his and he realized the referee was trying to separate the two
fighters. Kennedy stepped back and for the first time saw, really saw,
Malik Andrews, the man he was fighting. But before Kennedy could
take it all in, the referee motioned with his arms—Kennedy remembered too late the meaning—and Kennedy absorbed the punches again,
this time to the ribs, and then Malik Andrews whirled and kicked and
Kennedy thought someone had in fact this time knocked his head off his
shoulders.

He tried to remember everything Frank had told him, and the one
thing he could remember was that he needed to keep his hands up, so he
moved forward again, half-bent at the waist, his hands up around his
face, his elbows tucked in, trying to protect his ribs. The blows ricocheted
off his gloves and he knew he could defend himself, knew he could take
the occasional blow, and so he opened himself up a bit more, went on the
attack, and he relished the impact of his fist against another man's flesh.
Each time he connected, he grew stronger, and bulled his way forward,
backing the other man against the ropes and then delivering a series of
blows to the body, working the ribs, working the ribs, wearing the man
down, splitting him in two. And then the bell was ringing and he was
being directed back to his corner and he felt himself wobble, saw flashes,
and then the corner. He took a seat and felt the cold water from the
sponge on his face and he spit out his mouthpiece and tried to breathe, his
lungs shallow, needing air and needing it now.

When he came to, she was pounding on the door and shouting his name
and trying to push the door open—but something was in her way. Finally Kennedy realized it was his right shoulder—he was flat on his stomach on the floor of the small bathroom and his body was shaking, his
knees banging against the tile, and his shoulder was blocking the door.
He tried to remember her name, to say it aloud, to reassure her, but he
couldn't remember her name, and he wanted to cry. The room came back
into focus. The white ceramic sink. The toilet bowl. The towel rack. He
looked down the length of his naked body and realized that he had wet

himself, that he was lying in his own urine. He couldn't move. His body throbbed with pain. Kennedy told himself to just lie still, to collect his bearings, but the woman kept pounding.

Finally, he managed to mutter, "Stop. Stop."

She did. It grew quiet in the trailer except for the sound of the sewer pipes, the toilet tank refilling.

"What's wrong? Are you okay? Tell me you're okay."

Kennedy tried to figure out what had happened and how he could explain it. He looked around for blood, pressed his fingers against his lips, his nose, his scalp. He felt for wounds, gashes, broken bones, tears, holes.

"I think I passed out," he said. "Just give me a moment."

"Can I come in?" she asked.

"No. No. Just give me a second."

He didn't want her to see him like this, not this woman who was attracted to fighters.

"Do you want me to call an ambulance? Do you want me to call 9–1–1?"

"No," Kennedy said.

He forced himself to roll onto his side and then sit up. The dizziness subsided. He tried to prioritize the pain. He knew he needed to drink water. Maybe he was dehydrated. Maybe that was all. He crawled over to his gray cotton shorts, damp and cool with sweat, and managed to pull them back on without standing up. Already his collapse, the passing out, the pissing himself, the blood in his urine—had receded into the past. Slowly he climbed to his knees, pulled down a towel draped over the shower stall and dropped it over the small pool of urine on the tile floor. He used the sink to lever himself to his feet, then stepped on the towel to soak up the urine.

He stood at the sink, both hands firm on its rim. He waited for the world to slow down, to steady itself again. He dared not close his eyes even to blink. He turned on the cold water, just let it run for a couple minutes. He filled a small Dixie cup with water. He raised it to his lips. He drank. He did it again. Again. Again.

Frank stood in front of him, wild-eyed and nervous, cricking his neck from side to side. Frank was an Indian, though Kennedy could never remember what tribe. Kennedy owed his fight career to Frank. It was Frank who had convinced Kennedy to do this, eight weeks ago. They'd been seated at a table at Sunset Strip, watching the girls do their thing, which is to say, the girls were undressing in front of the men and shaking their tits and asses and offering lap dances for twenty bucks so they could feed and clothe their children. Kennedy was a sucker for single mothers. Kennedy had met Frank before but they'd never really talked. Frank asked what he was into and Kennedy said he didn't know. Frank suggested boxing, maybe hitting a heavy bag and jumping rope and sparring and knocking a few heads around. So, the following Monday night Kennedy was in the gym. Frank gave him pointers and told him he was a natural. Soon they had a goal and this was it, Fight Night at The Wildcat House, a mix of traditional boxing, kickboxing, and street scrum. Kennedy didn't know where Frank had learned all this fight stuff; he certainly didn't look like a fighter, too muscle-bound, too slow. But it was all up there in his head and he told Kennedy what to do and Kennedy did it. Jab. Punch. Counter. Move. Move. Move. Never stop moving.

So here was Frank on the big night, nervous, more nervous than Kennedy. Kennedy could see the sweat beading on Frank's brow.

"Relax," Kennedy said. He gestured toward the sweat.

Frank brushed it away. "Just warm in here," he said.

Kennedy stood, flexed his shoulders back and forth, bounced up and down on his tiptoes once, twice, three times. He felt Frank's nervous energy pass into him. He tried not to think about it.

"I just want you to know I appreciate all you done for me," Kennedy said. "It means a lot, you know."

"Fuck the sentimental bullshit, Kennedy. Just get in there and hit him hard a few times."

"I will."

"Get your money's worth."

"It only cost twenty to enter."

"Well, make sure you get twenty dollars worth of good hard hits."

Kennedy nodded. He tried to calculate how many good hard hits it would take—not just to win, but to put the guy on his back.

Kennedy examined the schedule: a straightforward, single-elimination bracket. There were sixteen fighters signed up in the heavy-weight division so it would take four fights to win it all. Kennedy had drawn Malik Andrews first, a man that Kennedy knew by reputation. Andrews had once played football for the university, nearly a decade ago, an undersized linebacker who blew out his knee early in his senior season and who had had to settle for local celebrity, appearing year after year in commercials for a local pawn shop. By the time Kennedy realized that if he won his first fight, he'd have to fight again right away—back-to-back fights—Frank had disappeared from sight, slipping through the crowd, which watched ambivalently as two undersized white kids danced around the ring, each occasionally flailing an arm toward the other, hitting nothing.

He told himself he didn't need a doctor. If you didn't need a doctor, it wasn't serious. Drink the water. Take some Tylenol. Ice the bruises. Apply heat for twenty minutes to the sore muscles. Rest. Above all, rest.

There was swelling around his right eye and cheek, a purplish-pink bruise rimmed with yellow. The skin around the other eye was red and puffy, and his jaw had the shadow of three days without a shave. His blondish hair was a mess, as though it hadn't been combed or washed in a week. It appeared thinner than usual on top, his scalp a whitish-pink that always reminded him of an infant's. He turned his head left and then right, and wondered if he would be able to tell if his brain was swollen. If only part of his brain was swollen, would he be able to see it here, in his bathroom mirror? He looked for bruises, purple-black marks on his skull. Was it broken? It felt like it was broken. He thought he would vomit, and leaned over the sink to wait for the acidic burn to rise up his throat. He could feel the capsules of Tylenol—all seven, all lucky seven—threatening to return. But nothing came. He spit into the sink and then cupped his hands beneath the flow of water and splashed it into his face.

When he opened the door, she was slumped against the opposite wall, her ass on the floor, knees against her chest, arms around her bare legs. Kennedy stepped into the narrow hallway and sat down across from her, avoiding her gaze.

"Sorry," he said. "I'm not a very good host."

He wanted her to laugh, but she didn't.

"Are you okay?" she asked.

"Define okay," he said.

Still she didn't laugh.

To answer her question, he wasn't sure where he should begin. In how many ways could he define himself as okay or not okay? He didn't think he was going to die. So that was something.

"Did I tell you what I was going to use the money for—if I had won tonight?"

"Yeah," she said. "On the drive over."

Kennedy nodded. He couldn't remember the drive.

"Did you drive?" he asked.

She looked up and Kennedy saw something in her gaze, though he couldn't sort it out. Not right now. Maybe he saw nothing. "You did, didn't you? I remember now," he said. But he still didn't remember.

"Yeah, I drove," she said. "You talked the whole time, about your little girl."

"Anna."

"Yeah, Anna. She's six, lives with her mother on the east side."

Kennedy nodded. He pointed down the hall, back into the living room.

"That's her," he said. "In those pictures."

The woman rose and she walked over to a card table that Kennedy had turned into a family shrine. On it were pictures of an elderly man and woman, a younger Kennedy and a little girl—now an infant, now a toddler, here a kindergartner, sometimes with teeth, sometimes with a smile, always with her father's blue eyes. The woman lifted a framed photo from the table and examined it closely. It was Kennedy and the girl in the park in midtown, the one with the old steam engine and a public swimming pool. She was on his shoulders, her small hands pressed against his forehead, mouth open, head thrown back in joy.

"I'm trying to get shared custody," Kennedy said. He wasn't certain if he'd already told her this. He wanted her to understand something about himself, though he wasn't certain what that was. "But I need to get my act together, show the judge I'm a good father. I mean, I am a good father. I just keep fucking up in other ways."

"A girl needs a good father," the woman said. She set the photograph back on the table. She looked around the rest of the living room, as though seeing it for the first time. And now Kennedy was embarrassed by its shabbiness, its cheap, second-hand furniture, the stained carpet, the dishes in the sink and on the counter and on the coffee table. The tear in the window screen above the kitchen sink, the one he always intended to repair. He was ashamed by the lack of order, the sense of indifference it reflected.

"I need to dust," Kennedy said.

This time, the woman laughed, though he had been serious. He needed to dust.

A curtain had been set up to create an impromptu locker room in one corner of the bar, and behind the curtain, fighters stripped down to their fight clothes, stretched out, had their muscles massaged by friends acting as trainers, and stood in front of a full-length mirror to shadowbox. Other fighters jumped rope in tight spaces or did jumping jacks or push-ups and sit-ups, trying to get the body loose, the muscles warm, to break a sweat before they stepped into the ring. Kennedy sat on the floor and unzipped his blue Goodwill duffel bag. He removed his gloves and his tape, a pair of used, red leather shoes with twenty eyelets that rose halfway up his calves. He'd bought them for fifteen bucks off Rodriguez at the gym. Rodriguez had been a semiprofessional boxer in Mexico when he was much younger, and he assured Kennedy that they were magical, that he would feel like he was floating on air if he wore them in the ring. Kennedy had bought them without ever trying them on, drawn to the color, a rich red that reminded him of adobe houses and Mexican girls at bullfights in Nogales. He had tried them on at home to make sure they'd fit and they did, though when he wore them around the trailer, while he made himself an omelet or drank a beer and listened to the radio, he didn't feel like he was floating. He just felt like he was wearing a pair of leather socks.

Kennedy pictured Malik Andrews in front of him, tried to generate animosity and rage toward Malik Andrews. But he couldn't. He'd always felt sorry for Andrews whenever he saw him on those commercials for the pawn shop. He wasn't half-bad in them, standing in front of the shop in a shirt and tie, the shirt looking like it would burst at the seams if Malik took a deep breath. He would smile affably into the camera and go through his lines, giving a half-punch of his right fist to punctuate the tag line: "There's nothing we won't buy or sell—Wildcat Pawn Shop." Kennedy wanted to rush out and sell something to the pawn shop, anything to spare Malik the humiliation. At least he could stop by and browse over the things they had for sale, not actually to buy anything, but maybe Malik would be there and they could talk a little football, talk about those glory days, the blocked punt he had against ASU his junior year, the fours sacks against Cal.

When Kennedy emerged from behind the curtain, he saw Claudia. She was wearing a tight black dress. Kennedy loved that about her. Two children. Thirty years old. And still. Look at that body. If that didn't provide incentive, Kennedy didn't know what would. It had been seven months since they'd seen each other and even longer since they'd last had sex, but when Kennedy saw her in that tight black dress, he knew she'd worn that dress for him and that this would be his night, this would be a new beginning for the both of them, together. Fuck her husband. He was a bastard. And he was still in Mexico. She wasn't going back. Not with her kids. Not where the husband could get his hands on her kids.

Kennedy worked his way toward her. There were college kids in catalogue freshness; businessmen in black suits with gold ties and gold bracelets and gold rings, cell phones hooked to their snakeskin belts; black women and Hispanic men from the barrio in oversized neon football jerseys and matching caps; dye-bottle blondes in micro-skirts and too much makeup, low-cut tops revealing silicone and lace. The crowd milled around the ring that had been erected in the center of the bar, half in practiced poses of indifference, the other half leaning forward and straining to cheer on their friends and coworkers. Kennedy moved deliberately through the crowd, aware of his body, of its physicality, more aware of his body today than he could ever recall. The people around him stepped back, giving him room. He liked the feeling of his body, the tension in his arms, the strength in his legs, the lightness of his feet. He felt buoyant, the air filling his lungs, and imagined himself a butterfly slipping through the net of people. He could almost believe in this moment that there wasn't anyone in the building that he could not destroy with his bare hands.

He tapped her on the shoulder with his taped fist. She turned and smiled.

"Hello, Kennedy," she said.

Kennedy thanked her for coming, said nothing else mattered now. He was so glad to see her. He told her she looked beautiful. He tried to forget what she had told him the last night they had been together. They were both lying naked in his bed in the back room of the trailer. They were both huddled under the covers, keeping warm on a cool desert night, the heat moving back and forth between their bodies. She had told him she didn't think he was man enough to handle the mess she was in— the INS, the children, the threats from her husband in Hermosillo. She said all these things in English, spoke clearly and confidently, so much better than she had six months before, the first time they had lain in his bed after sex.

"You're gonna win," she told Kennedy.

"Give me a good luck kiss," he said. He raised his taped fist to his cheek and bent over. She hesitated, but then did as he said, a quick touch of her lips to his cheek. In that brief moment, he remembered with long-ing the touch of her fingers on his skin in the morning, tracing the ridge of his spine up and down his back, and then he allowed the thought to pass from his mind.

"I'll be thinking of you in the ring," he said, though he knew she was the last thing he could afford to think about in the ring if he wanted to win the five hundred bucks.

She blushed like a young girl. She smiled. "Kill 'em," she said. Kennedy touched her forehead with his thumb, then backed away, bumping into another competitor who was exiting the prep area, a silk robe wrapped around his shoulders.

Kennedy had run into Claudia's sister Mishoul the previous week at Safeway and had invited them both. He didn't think either would come. And yet, here she was. It was a sign. It had to be a sign.

The woman told him he should lie down. She led him into the bedroom with its unmade, narrow double-bed, the mattress cover peeled back to reveal a worn pink mattress. The drawers to the dresser were half-opened, the closet overloaded. Socks, underwear, sweat-stained T-shirts spilled from the hamper. A punching bag sat in the corner. The only light in the room came from the hallway. On the wall above the bed hung a wooden crucifix, the agonized figure of Christ painted a ghastly red and yellow and brown. Kennedy had purchased it from a street vendor in Nogales, an emaciated woman with a small, dark-skinned child, its gender indistinguishable in the rags it wore.

"Are you Catholic?" the woman asked.

Kennedy sat on the edge of the bed and then lay back. He dragged his body toward the wall, trying to make room for her to join him. But she remained standing.

"Not really," Kennedy said.

On the dresser there was a golden Buddha. Over the window hung a series of crystals, dull and clear in the darkness. From the ceiling above the bed, a dream weaver twisted slowly, like a child's mobile. There was a poster of Gandhi and another of John Lennon. A pair of plush, black dice hung from the corner of a mirror above the dresser. A light saber.

"You can never have too much good karma," he said.

"Do you like it out here?" the woman asked.

"Yeah, I do," he said. "It's quiet."

He had moved here nearly two years ago from D.C., trying to start over, trying to get closer to his daughter somehow. He found this trailer in a wildcat subdivision out near Pictured Rocks. Though it didn't have much in the way of amenities, he took a certain pride in its austerity, occasionally thinking of himself as a postmodern monk who deprived himself of the distractions of the material world to get closer to the real. Some mornings he would rise at 4:30 when the desert was still dark and cool, even in the summer, and run for thirty or forty minutes along the dirt road that passed his trailer. He would accelerate on the down slopes into the dry washes, then labor to come back up the other side. But most mornings he slept as late as he could before driving into the city to his job at the Circle K, corner of 6th and Park.

Kennedy told her these things, told her how he'd disappointed his parents. He told her how he wanted to go back to college, get his degree. "It's never too late," she said. He talked and talked and he wondered if he was talking too much. But she seemed content to listen and so he told her some more. But there was something he was forgetting. It wasn't lost to him. Not yet. It was something he knew he had once remembered, had remembered for a long time. It was something he knew he needed to remember, but right now he couldn't.

"I want to tell you something, but I can't remember it," he said.

"It's okay," she said. "I'm sure it's not important."

"No, it is. I know it is."

"Okay. Take your time then."

"I need to tell you now. Before I forget it completely."

"Okay. Tell me."

"I can't. I can't remember everything."

"Tell me what you can remember."

Here is what Kennedy wanted to tell her. The number of the hospital room. The name of the hospital. The scent of the room. He tried to remember the doctor's name, the doctor's face, any of the nurses. He tried to remember the clothes the infant wore, the clipboards at the end of the bed, the colors of the wall. The tiny hands, the texture of the skin, the shape of the skull. Were there flowers? What kind? He tried to remember the weather that day. For a moment it was sunny and 85, and then gray and wintry, a thin layer of snow on the ground outside. All certainty of the memory seemed to be gone. It had been February, hadn't it? He had this written down, somewhere. He remembered this detail and clung to it as to a life raft. He tried to build another memory upon this memory, to create links. He hoped that one detail would open the door to another. He saw the memory as series of doors he must walk through. If only he could find and open the first door. Manage to unlock it.

Here's what Kennedy was able to tell her. That he hadn't been there for his daughter's birth. Even then, at the very beginning when everything was still possible, when all good things could happen, he'd messed up.

"I need to explain," he said.

"Explain what?"

"Who I am."

"You don't have to explain that."

"Yes I do."

"But why? Why this? Why now?"

"Because I don't want you to think I'm something I'm not."

She laughed. Kennedy smiled though he didn't know why she had laughed or why he was smiling.

He had been seventeen. He remembered this. He had had to go with his father to visit Sienna's parents and to tell them that he was the father. There had been anger and tears. There had been threats. They had sat in the kitchen. There had been coffee. No one drank the coffee. He felt the doors open, pushed through to the next.

He imagined a hospital, like one he'd seen on TV. And a baby. It was a sunny summer afternoon. It began to come clear to him. A woman in a bed, handshakes and congratulations. A table with greeting cards and a blue vase with yellow flowers. Daisies. Someone asked him the name of the child. He said, Anna. Beautiful Anna.

"I used to remember more of it. Lots more," he said.

"You can't remember everything," she said.

There was a conscious moment when Kennedy ceded that he was no longer capable of defending himself. It didn't come in the first fight, which he won by unanimous decision over Malik Andrews, and it didn't come in the second fight, which he won by TKO when the other fighter twisted awkwardly and tore up his knee. It came in the semifinal round against Slammin' Sammy, a 6-foot-2, 245-pound Adonis who worked as a prison guard at the state penitentiary in Florence. Kennedy raised his gloved hands in front of his face and just tried to hold them there while Sammy hit him again and again in the ribs and in the kidneys. Kennedy tried to remember every prayer he'd ever prayed, tried to appeal to every god or spirit or force within hearing range, tried to call up all his remaining good karma, whatever he had left, whatever might be possible to get him through this, to keep on his feet, to keep him from getting killed. He didn't even care if he won now, didn't even care if he made a respectable showing. He decided that he'd been selfish to want to win it all, that had been his mistake—too much pride—and this was his lesson, his payment, his purgatory. He took a blow to the side of the head. His jaw snapped. He thought that it might come unhinged, just drop off his face. He saw silver stars and blue lights and then he was in his corner and Frank was in his face, telling him that he was doing great, great, just great, just hang in there, keep the hands up, look to go on the offensive. Then Frank shoved the mouthpiece back in and Kennedy stumbled forward toward the center of the ring. Sammy met him there and hit him again and again and again.

By the time Kennedy hit the canvas, tipping sideways like a ship listing to sea, he had surrendered himself to the fates, his hands at his side, his body an open target, a sack of flesh and bones.

In the parking lot, they leaned against Rodriguez's tricked-out Cutlass Supreme, the music loud, a Southwestern mix of rap and ska and mariachis. The sun had long retreated behind the mountains to the west and the air had begun to cool. Someone offered that it had been 105 that afternoon. They passed around bottles of vodka and Jack, some dope, and Kennedy drank and smoked his fair share, content to dull the pain of the bruises and the cuts with the oldest medicine known to man. They told Kennedy he had fought valiantly, that he had proved himself in the ring. How long he had stood there, how much punishment he had taken. None of them could have lasted as long, none of them could've taken more than one or two, maybe three punches, before boom—down, they would've hit the canvas. But not Kennedy. Our own Rocky, someone said. Kennedy tried to distinguish one voice from another, but he was still having difficulty, everything blurred, sights and space, light and dark, sounds and silence, nothing quite in focus. He knew Claudia was there— she had kissed him on the cheek, and Rodriguez—Kennedy knew it was his car—and there were two or three others or maybe five or six, Kennedy didn't really know. Who had gone home? Who had remained? People kept walking up and walking away and they kept saying his name. El Presidente. They touched him on the elbow or on the bicep and Kennedy would shiver, try to nod.

Mishoul was there too. During the fights, she had been in the row behind Claudia. Kennedy had seen her just as he was stepping into the ring. He'd dated her before Claudia and briefly again after, if you could call what they did dating. She was two years younger than Claudia, and if anyone had forced him to answer, he'd admit that Mishoul had been a better fuck, more adventurous, more willing to do everything and to do it anywhere, but she also could be a bitch, highly demanding. Her moods shifted like the fault lines of California.

Kennedy told everyone he wanted to go to Sunset Strip to watch the pretty girls, to see them shake their tits, but everyone just laughed as though it was a tremendous joke.

The woman lifted the dress above her head and slipped her arms through the sleeves, then allowed it to slide back down over her body. Kennedy turned away, embarrassed that she might catch him staring. He pulled the damp bed sheet against his body.

"I can't remember your name," he said. "I'm sorry."

"That's okay," she said. "I never told you."

"You didn't?"

"No."

"Why not?"

"It's easier that way," she said. "Less to remember. Less to forget."

"Why wouldn't I want to remember your name?"

"Because it's not important. A name is just a name. Sounds. Letters. A word. There are lots of words."

He tried to guess her name. Melissa, Sarah, Sadie, Katrina, Elizabeth, Corinna, Valerie. Claudia. Mishoul. Anna. But he realized she was none of these women.

"I'm a good father," he said.

She touched his neck with her forefinger. Drew a line down it. She leaned forward and kissed him. Kennedy kissed her back. She kissed him fiercely. He thought she would swallow his tongue.

"Say my name," Kennedy said.

But she refused.

Kennedy stood in front of the toilet again, the stream of urine filling the toilet bowl in fits and starts. All that water and Gatorade, all that liquor. Just when he thought he was finished, as he was shaking himself off, he saw the spot of blood drip into the toilet and then another, its bright red still a shock. For a moment he thought of the artist who had filled a jar with his own piss and then dropped a crucifix inside. This is what was missing, Kennedy thought. The blood. The blood in the urine.

Before the woman had left, Kennedy had apologized.

"I'm sorry I couldn't make love," he said.

"But we did," she said.

When he was finished, he pulled his shorts up and knotted them. He walked through the trailer with its narrow rooms and its cheap paneled walls, and he opened the front door and sat on the metal two-step grate that passed as his front stoop. It was still dark outside though to the east there was just the first hint of morning light. The sound of traffic from the nearby interstate highway drifted over the saguaros and ocotillo, cars and trucks bound north for Phoenix and south to Tucson. The sky was clear and full of stars and against the horizon Kennedy could see the darker outlines of the surrounding mountain ranges, each distinct in its aspect. In the darkness, Kennedy shaped the words with his tongue, pushed the sounds from his mouth, spoke them into being: the Tortolitas, the Santa Ritas, the Rincons, the Santa Catalinas. He said the names again—Tortolitas, Santa Ritas, Rincons, Santa Catalinas. Just kept saying—Tortolitas, Santa Ritas, Rincons, Santa Catalinas—as though the mountains and the names were forever.

How We Fought the
War on Terrorism

I didn't belong there. I knew this, even then, that last week in August when the air hung like a wet towel on your skin, the basement of Williams Hall a musty, stale, windowless space, metal desk frames nailed to the tile floor. I didn't belong there. A mix of traditional college students looking for an easy grade, single mothers in search of an outlet for creative expression, and science fiction aficionados with intricate worlds of their own design packed into three-ring binders. But the economy had gone sour. When my brother cut my hours at his landscaping business, he apologized and assured me it was only temporary. My wife, mostly to cheer me up, I think, told me to take a class. The travel agency was doing well; we could afford it. It was my brother who told me to sign up for the writing class. He was friends with the professor, Colin Louis—we plowed his drive in the winter—so I did.

I'd always wanted to be an author. When I was a kid, it was the height of the Cold War, and though I lived in a small Midwestern town of no strategic value, I lay awake nights, listening for the sound of Soviet tanks on Main Street, the clap-clap of a thousand leather boots on the sidewalk outside Bisel's 5-and-Dime. I wrote stories, and in these stories, I stood atop the roof of Bartholomew's Shoe Store, a solitary figure against a lead sky, wounded, bleeding, yet fighting for freedom and country, God and Mother, the last defender of the last domino in the Free World. But I grew up, discovered girls, trucks, football. The Cold War ended. I met Grace. We married. Our daughter Rachel was born. We bought a two-bedroom bungalow over on Palmer Avenue, just beyond the IGA and just before the railroad tracks. I went to work for my brother—lawns and landscape work from spring to fall, snow plowing parking lots and private driveways in the winter.

Still, I didn't belong there. I only wanted to tell a good story, to make people feel good inside, maybe laugh. I believed I was a good father, a good husband. The rest didn't matter.

On that first night, a Tuesday, Dr. Louis explained how the class functioned. It was a workshop. We'd exchange stories ahead of time, read the stories and discuss them the following week. The author, he explained, doesn't get to say a word during these discussions. The author, Dr. Louis said, is dead.

He laughed as he said this and so too did some of the others. I didn't get it.

It's just a theory, he said, patient with my ignorance. Once the reader has the text—the story—the author doesn't matter. Meaning resides between the reader and the text. So when we talk about each other's stories, the author will remain silent.

He pinched his thumb and forefinger and moved them from left to right across his lips.

When I arrived home, I told all this to Grace. She slumped in a chair at the kitchen table, beautiful in her casual repose, drinking tea and winking at me. She acted as though everything I said was fresh and new, and the more I talked, the more enthusiastic I became. I knew she wanted to go to bed and get naked, but now I was feeling witty and verbose, more than a little inspired.

She stood and came to me, placed her toes against mine and rose on her tiptoes. She wrapped her arms around my neck, and whispered so Rachel couldn't hear: Let's have sex, she said. This author ain't dead yet.

Every afternoon for the next week, when I arrived home from work, I sat at the computer and wrote. I was full of ideas, every one original. I wrote a story about growing up on the farm. I wrote a story in which the narrator becomes a fabulously successful businessman and buys the entire nation of Kazhakstan and turns it into a vacation paradise. I wrote a story about a dog that knows the mind of God and tries to warn the world of impending doom. I tore all these up because I knew nothing of farms or Kazhakstan or God.

Then I wrote a story about Rachel's birth. It was only three pages, but I liked it. I changed the names, but you could probably tell. There was too much love for the baby not to be real.

The second Tuesday of September we did not have class. Everyone sat at home and stared at the television screen where the World Trade Center collapsed again and again into rubble. A gray cloud, then rubble. Fire, smoke, gray cloud, rubble. Grace and I watched it over and over. We sent Rachel to bed early. We agreed she shouldn't see this thing, this awful thing, this death thing. We closed the door to her room and kept the sound low. We called Grace's parents in Kalamazoo, and we called my parents in Sturgis, forty minutes south. None of us knew anyone in New York—we didn't think so anyway, but you never know, someone could have gone there for a visit, and it's all so awful, so beyond our imaginations, something right out of Hollywood, but real. Grace and I watched the images over and over again, every few hours a new angle, but still the same thing. Someone compared it to Pearl Harbor. War has come and Americans will never be the same again, they said. We heard this a hundred times. We will never be the same again. When Grace and I realized this—everything now was repetition, nothing more would happen that night—we went to bed and made love, hard and furious, like it might be the last time ever, though neither of us would ever say anything like that and neither of us really believed it yet.

In the morning, my brother and I dug our fingers into the soil and worked hard, like it was our patriotic duty, our own middle finger to the terrorists. We kept a radio close by and listened to talk shows all day. There was a fierce surge of patriotism. It was like we were getting our marching orders. We would bomb them all, we would show no fear, we would not back down. Ordinary men and women were hailed as heroes.

Everyone loved New York. We were all in this together. We were all Americans. At lunch, in the cab of my truck, I wrote a letter to the editor. I demanded justice and retribution and revenge. I tore it up and wrote another, then tore that one up too. But it was okay. Lots of letters would say what I would've said. They would say it more poetically.

At the travel agency where Grace worked, the phones rang off the hook, everyone nervous, canceling travel plans and seeking refunds. Grace urged her clients to remain calm. On her lunch break, she drove to the Red Cross and tried to donate blood. The lines were too long and she told them she'd be back in the evening even though she hated needles and fainted at the sight of blood. When she returned to the agency, a dark-skinned man was standing in the middle of the lobby, and he was gesturing toward the street and shouting in a language no one could understand. Everyone was panicked. One woman had hidden beneath her desk, another was calling 9–1–1, and a third was standing on top of her desk and yelling to the man, "Just calm down! Just calm down!" No one was answering the phones, which continued to ring. By the time the police arrived, someone had finally figured out that the man had car troubles and needed to use a phone, and that he was Mexican, not Arab anyway, but then the police discovered he was in the country illegally and so they still hauled him off to jail.

In the afternoon, Rachel came home from school in tears, dragging her tiny pink backpack along the sidewalk. Strands of her curly blonde hair had sprung free from the braids and barrettes.

I don't want to die! I don't want to die! she said over and over.

At school, the teacher had gathered the kids in a circle. Everyone talked about the bad thing those people did, how they hated our country and how lots of people died and what a sad thing it was. Some kids were scared and started to cry, but the teacher assured them that everything was fine. They were safe. Their mommies and their daddies and their teachers and the police officers and even the President would keep them from harm.

Rachel said she didn't cry at all and then on the bus ride home, a bigger boy, an older boy, a boy she had never seen before, had turned in his seat to face her and he said, They'll kill the little girls first!

She started to sob again. I wrapped my arms around her and pulled her close, shocked by how small her body felt against mine. I petted her head with my hand, trying to soothe her fears. I told her they don't kill little girls; God won't allow it. The boy, he's just a boy, he doesn't know what he's talking about. She listened and her sobs gradually turned to whimpers and finally her whimpers ceased and she wiped the sleeve of her shirt across her cheeks and looked up, our nearly identical brown eyes meeting. For a moment I thought she almost believed me.

An uneasiness settled over the campus. Students gathered around the quad, uncertain of the proper response. Some wore American flags pinned to shirts or backpacks, others held two fingers aloft asking for peace. From a small plywood platform, speakers assured the Arab-Americans and Muslim Americans among us that they were not the targets of our anger. In turn, the Muslim students insisted that Islam was a religion of peace. A faculty member, a woman from the physics department, criticized the President for calling this a war. Students and professors knelt in prayer, lit candles, and read poems. Everyone tried hard to avoid the mistakes of history—of McCarthy, Vietnam, El Salvador, the Persian Gulf War. We wanted to be sensitive warriors.

In the hallway during a break, Lydia—a young woman who sat beside me and smelled of patchouli and cigarette smoke—distributed a poem that she had written and asked for our opinions. She wanted to know what we thought. Be honest, she said.

In the poem, the hijacked planes become giant phallic symbols and the Trade Towers become two virgins that are raped by the planes, the male hegemony of violence against women enacted en masse, yet one more rape propagated upon society by men, terrorists raping the national body.

No one knew what to say. After all, it was poetry and it contained the word "fuck." Most of the students read the poem in the hallway and then stuffed it into their backpacks or folded it in quarters and slipped it into their jeans pockets. Lydia retrieved a silver metal cigarette case from her purse, removed a cigarette, lit it, and began to smoke. She told us again to be honest—come on, you won't hurt my feelings; it's just something I threw together, she said—but I knew she wanted to be told that it's brilliant, insightful, a bulldozer of a poem.

You make it sound like the terrorists just wanted a good fuck, I said.

It's a metaphor, she said.

It's a sick metaphor, I said.

Don't shout, she said.

I'm not shouting.

But I was shouting. We both were. Everyone else retreated to the far corners of the hallway or slipped back into the room. No one wanted to be collateral damage.

When I came home, I told all this to Grace.

She made all the men in the class feel like rapists, I said. Like we were somehow responsible, like it's men against women. Like everything is men against women. Like all men think about is sex. It's not always about sex.

Grace responded that it was a very emotional time and people were scared and trying to figure things out, trying to come to grips with the tragedy. They want to find a way to explain it, to find words that can express it, she said.

It sounded to me like my wife was agreeing with the woman and so I asked if her if she thought the woman was right.

It's not that it's right or wrong, she said. She went upstairs to tuck Rachel into bed. I knew she thought I was wrong.

That night, it was warm in our bedroom and we lay atop the bedcovers, Grace with her leg across mine. She nibbled at my ear and held my hand with both of hers. Then she brushed her hand across my bare chest and down toward my groin. I turned and rolled her over onto her back and slipped my body between her legs. We did the things we'd done a thousand times, lips against lips, flesh against flesh, and she became aroused but I did not, she became wet, but I did not become hard. We kept kissing, touching, and fondling, and finally I apologized, and rolled back over to my side of the bed. I reached down and pulled the bedsheet over us. Grace asked if everything was okay. I said, yes, just tired, stressed from the day and the week. I apologized again.

In the darkness of the bedroom, I kept seeing those two airplanes, first one and then the other, then the one and then the other.

I got out of bed. In the living room, I turned on the TV and watched reruns of the prime-time cable news talk shows. I muted the sound, enabled the closed captions. I changed channels and changed channels again. Later, Grace joined me on the couch. We pulled a cotton throw around us. She slid one arm around my shoulders and placed the other across my chest. We watched in silence. Eventually, she fell asleep with her head on my shoulder. I did not sleep. On every damn channel, it was the same damn thing.

The note from the school arrived on Day-Glo orange stationery, folded in half and safety-pinned to Rachel's white T-shirt. It expressed its condolences to those that had lost friends and loved ones in the tragedies of September 11, and then it outlined emergency procedures that were in place should such a situation arise here. The note encouraged us to talk with our children in age-appropriate ways, to be honest, but not to unnecessarily frighten them. We should pay close attention to our children and watch for any sudden shifts in their behavior. Most importantly, we were to assure them that they were safe and protected and that they should not live in fear either at home or at school.

That evening we watched a celebrity fundraiser on television. In tears Grace called the toll-free number on the screen and authorized a $200 donation to the New York Police and Fire Widows' and Children's Fund. "Charge it to our credit card," she said.

On Sunday, we attended church for the first time in months though the service was more like a patriotic rally than a time to worship God. We sang all the patriotic hymns—*The Battle Hymn of the Republic, The Star-Spangled Banner, God of Our Fathers*—and we recited the *Pledge of Allegiance,* hands over stricken hearts. Digital images of people from around the world gathered in prayer for America were displayed on the video screens at the front of either side of the auditorium. A red, white, and blue ribbon draped around the cross that hung above the choir loft. From the pulpit, the pastor assured us that God remained in control, and the pastor encouraged us to seek refuge in the arms of the Almighty in our hour of need. He spoke of the opportunity for spiritual reflection, renewal, and revival in a nation that had turned its heart from God. Around us, people wept and held hands and whispered, amen, amen, amen.

Later that afternoon, Grace decided to organize a Bake Sale for America. She called her friends, her co-workers, the Women's Chamber of Commerce. She would place an ad in the paper, get permission from the local bank to hold it on Saturday in its parking lot. The manager, a friend of hers from high school, said he'd arrange for a tent, in case of bad weather, and he'd place signs on the front doors inviting people to participate.

We have to do something, she said.

Every day we learned another way that they could kill us. Trucks that haul hazardous waste. Nerve agents drifting through the air vents. My neighbor, Lester, told me the things the government and the media would not. It's worse, he said, than you know.

He stood on my front steps late in the evening. A large man with a long, gray-brown beard that fanned out from his double chin, he wore overalls and work boots and spoke in an animated hush, as though someone might overhear him. These are the things you're not supposed to know, he said, and if you know them you're not supposed to say.

I nodded. I wanted him to think we are in this together.

Do you know, he said, that twenty-five suitcase nuclear weapons are missing from our arsenal? Do you know, he said, that the terrorists were only eight centimeters off from bringing down the Trade Center in '93? Do you know, he said, that our forces took on Israel in mock battles last year and got their asses whupped?

My neighbor learned all this from the Internet and short-wave radio and people he had met in his travels—a man who worked in procurement for the Air Force, a former Russian diplomat who now vacations in Miami, a military intelligence expert who once worked for the Israelis. I had no idea what Lester did for a living. He came and went as he pleased, it seemed. He claimed to be retired. I knew he once had a wife and a daughter—he admitted this much, in a moment of weakness perhaps, but he said no more of them. He drew connections for me between the CIA, Saudi sheiks, Moscow, Beijing, the oil industry, and the *Exxon Valdez*. I wanted him to be wrong. I wanted him to be a paranoid whacko, but I had no counterevidence to offer. Watergate? Iran-Contra? Bay of Pigs? Child's play, he said. He asked me if I'd ever read the Red Trident Report and if the numbers 12 and 4 and 68 meant anything to me.

When I said no, he just nodded, leaned back and stroked his beard. See, he said. See.

We could not find Rachel. Grace called her to dinner and received no reply. The dining room table was set and the ice in the glasses had begun to melt. I had made dinner, baked chicken, potatoes, and a garden salad. Grace walked through the kitchen and opened the backdoor and called Rachel again. She stepped into the backyard. I told her I'd check the front.

I walked through the living room to the front of the house. Rachel's pink backpack rested against an end table and her blue spring jacket was draped over the back of the couch. In the background, Peter Jennings provided the latest updates on the events of the day.

I opened the front door and stepped outside onto the porch. I looked up and down the street, still holding a serving spoon for the potatoes. The somber light of late evening lingered over the neighborhood and a faint breeze scraped leaves across the cement surface of our drive. On the sidewalk opposite, Mr. Hopson walked Oswald, his aging golden retriever, and the Meyer boys maneuvered their skateboards to avoid fallen walnuts. Lester had climbed atop a stepladder to replace a burned-out light bulb over his front door. When he saw me, he waved and I waved back. I was reminded that I liked this neighborhood with its sidewalks and its driveways, its porches and porch swings and the park at the end of the street. It was a neighborhood of stable single-family homes made with wood and brick, a neighborhood of basketball hoops and garage sales, oak trees with thick trunks and deep roots. The lawns were well kept and the fences merely ornamental.

Still, there was no sign of Rachel. I tried to remember if she had said she was going outside to play, maybe down to the park. I tried to remember if I had heard any cars stop or voices outside the house. But I could not recall. Maybe I just wasn't paying attention. I came back inside.

The evening news had gone to commercial and I stepped across the room to shut off the television. That's when I saw the toes of her black patent leather shoes peeking from beneath the curtain that draped the window that looked into Lester's yard. I nearly laughed, and then I wasn't certain if I should be angry with her for not answering the call to dinner or amused by this impromptu game of hide-and-seek. I was still caught in my parental ambivalence when I pulled back the curtain and found Rachel, eyes closed as tightly as she could muster, her fists clenched at her side, and her whole body shaking like a solitary leaf in a harsh, autumn wind. I knelt down in front of her and touched her shoulder with my hand and she screamed. My heart constricted.

Rachel, I said. It's okay.

She opened her eyes, still screaming, and then threw herself into my arms, still screaming. I tried to comfort her, told her everything was all right and asked her what was wrong and whispered in her ear, shush—shush—shush. It's okay, it's okay, it's okay. I looked back over my shoulder at Grace who stood behind me, mouth open, hand on her chest, and I saw the same fear that rose from deep within me.

Grace slid her hand between my legs and wrapped her fingers around my cock, but it lay limp and soft against the inside of my thigh. She stroked it, sucked it, played with it, and I tried to concentrate on everything that she did, then tried not to think about it at all, but the more I tried not to think about it, the worse it seemed, and the worse it seemed, the more I thought about it. She lit candles and massaged oils deep into my skin. She asked me what I wanted and I told her I didn't know, I didn't know what was wrong, something must be wrong, but I didn't know what it was.

She kissed me, touched me again, but all I could see were the towers and the planes and the fire and gray clouds, everything collapsing, everything collapsed.

No one liked my story. They hated it. We sat around the long wooden table and we agonized in silence. The professor sat at the head of the table and I sat opposite him, and in-between us, my classmates could think of nothing good to say and so they said as little as possible. I was not allowed to speak and so I alternated between doodles in the margins of my copy of the story and glances to my classmates, imploring them to speak! Speak! Speak! Say something! Somebody! The professor kept trying to lead them into conversation about character and point of view, but he met a reticence borne of some mix of kindness, embarrassment, uncertainty, and self-preservation.

The few comments were fragmented, disjointed, indirect.

They were not certain it was really a story. There's no conflict, Stacy said. Kordell said he was sometimes confused by awkward sentence structures. Dr. Louis asked him for examples and Kordell rattled off four and was on his way to five before Dr. Louis cut him off. Kristin wanted to know why we didn't know the wife's name. The narrator only refers to her as his wife.

It's like she's his possession or something, Kristin said.

Dr. Louis examined my story as it lay in front of him, like a disease for which there was no cure.

Then Lydia, who had sat through the entire conversation with her arms crossed, slumped back in her chair, leaned forward and asked if we could talk about the narcissism of the narrator.

The what? I said.

Dr. Louis raised a finger to his lips and looked at me.

Narcissism, Lydia said. He's stuck on himself.

He is not, I said.

Mr. Regan, Dr. Louis said, looking at me again, only this time harder, his finger pressed against his pale lips.

The author, I reminded myself, is dead.

Lydia thought I was a sexist pig. She talked about the narrator, the man with the camcorder in the delivery room, the man who talked about the birth as if it had been something where he'd done most of the work, a man who thought he deserved most of the credit, but I knew she realized the narrator was me, the narcissist, the pig. I was not a sympathetic character; I did not come to some understanding of myself or the world; there was no redemption for my flaws.

When she finished, Dr. Louis said nothing, only flipped one more time through the brief three pages as though maybe, just maybe, he could find a positive note upon which to finish our discussion, maybe a word he could praise for its creative spelling. But all he said was, Good, good. A good start. Thanks, Mr. Regan.

After class, Lydia pursued me through the quad, calling after me to wait. A light mist fell upon the darkened campus and around us a group of fraternity guys shouted to each other as they winged Frisbees toward a distant lamppost. When Lydia reached me, she was breathing harder than I thought she should be, but her mood was conciliatory. She told me a few people from class were meeting for drinks, a chance to kick back and get to know each other, talk bullshit. I told her I didn't know if I was into that. Then she told me it was okay what I said about her poem. She admitted it was a little over the top, crass even, all those emotions that she just didn't know what to do with.

I sorted through her words and phrases as I watched a Frisbee ding the lamppost and heard the frat guys cheer. She was smarter than me and we both knew it and so she could be so generous. Thank you for the invitation, I said, and for accepting my unoffered apology, but I already have a wife.

I turned and walked away.

Rachel memorized the Pledge of Allegiance. To Rachel's lunchbox, Grace affixed a sticker of the U.S. flag and another that said I LUV U. From Kmart we bought a crisp, new American flag to fly from the empty flagpole in our front yard. Grace forwarded patriotic e-mails to everyone we knew, and on a whim delivered a double-chocolate cake to the police station. She took to wearing a silver cross her grandmother gave her for her 13th birthday, and she joined a group of women from the Baptist church in a weekly prayer walk. In the evenings, they gathered together and moved from house to house, stopping in front of each to "pray a shield of God's protection" around the home and its occupants. To the refrigerator in our kitchen, Grace attached a map of the town and tracked the group's progress with a yellow highlighter as it moved block by block.

We dined out more often, to lend our support, in whatever small way possible, to the rebuilding of America. We forsook home-cooked meals for platters of chicken fingers and coleslaw, mushroom melts and steak fries. We endured wilting lettuce and overcooked hamburgers, sloppy service and empty calories, to support our local business community. We bought dessert and tipped well.

One night, Grace drove to Kalamazoo to the mall and bought two new dresses, a new top, and new shoes for herself, and for Rachel, she bought a Christmas-worth of school supplies, clothes, shoes, tights, and dolls. She came home with a new drill for me, though I didn't really need it, and a bright red America United sweatshirt that she insisted would fit me.

I didn't protest. I'd never been to war, never had to fight terrorism before, and Grace seemed better at it than me, seemed to know what we were supposed to be doing—she'd been watching TV, the cable news channels, and reading the newspapers. Everyone at the travel agency thought it was wonderful that she'd painted a large American flag in the front window.

And then one night I was doing the budget, totaling our expenses for the week and for the month. Everything was all haywire since her business was down and I was only working part-time now and we were trying to do our best for America, to keep the economy rolling. I said this to Grace, but she wouldn't have any of it.

We haven't been spending any more than usual, she said. We're just maintaining. We're not hiding in a hole.

I pointed to the receipts spread across the kitchen table, its own form of patriotism.

You're being hysterical, she said. The fear-mongering has gotten to you.

I'm only being practical, I said. The numbers don't lie.

Suddenly she raised her hands above her head and screamed, WE CAN'T . . . LET . . . THE TERRORISTS . . . WIN!

This is what they want! she screamed. To destroy our way of life!

We still have to the pay the bills, I said.

She shook her head. I was betraying my country, betraying her.

We found Rachel beneath the bed, in the closet, locked in the bathroom. We coaxed her from beneath the bed, we sat with her in the closet, we picked the lock to the bathroom, and when we asked her what was wrong, she said, Nothing.

Why were you under the bed? Because Radar wanted to be.

Why were you in the closet? I couldn't find my shoes.

Why did you lock the bathroom door? It locked itself.

She stroked Radar, the brown-and-white Beanie Baby cow that had become her constant companion. I told her Radar had no need to be scared, that we—Grace, Rachel, and I—would protect him, keep him from harm, that no one would hurt him. He is safe here, I said.

Rachel learned quickly, it seemed. She learned to act as though everything was fine. She played with her dolls. She ran through the house, skipping and counting to ten or saying the alphabet, as far as she could go, saying it over and over, and we breathed more easily, smiled to each other, assured ourselves that we were doing well, children are resilient. Then later we found her curled in the lazy Susan, asleep, all the boxes of rice and canned goods stacked on the counter above to make room for her little body.

Grace told me to come to bed. I told her I couldn't. I needed to write.

This is how writers work, I said. They get inspired and they have to write before everything slips back into the subconscious.

So she waited for hours alone in the bedroom while I sat in the study and stared into the white space of the computer monitor. I wrote nothing. On the Internet there were stories about death fucks, people fucking like they might die tomorrow, people fucking while watching the towers collapse, people fucking in the shadows of the rubble. In fear, people turn to sex.

I allowed myself to fall asleep in my chair or on the couch or even on the floor. When Grace awakened me, at three or at four, the room chilled and dark, and urged me to come to bed—the comfort of a mattress, a soft pillow, bedcovers—I acted disoriented, exhausted, wasted, as though I would not even remember this moment in the morning.

The principal of the school called Grace at work. They had found Rachel hiding in a trash bin behind the cafeteria. The principal wanted us to come pick her up. She smelled like yesterday's school lunch.

When I arrived, Grace was already seated in the principal's office, holding Rachel's hand. Rachel's feet dangled high above the floor. A pungent odor rose from where she sat. Her head was down, her chin on her chest. She thought she was in trouble. The adults in the crowded office— myself and Grace, the principal, Rachel's teacher, and the school counselor—thought she was in trouble, too, but it was a different kind of trouble, something deeper and more permanent than a spanking or a timeout in the corner or a loss of dessert privileges.

When we asked her questions, she answered them—she knew to respect adults, her teachers and her parents, to not lie, but to tell them what they wanted to hear. I don't want to die, she said. She said this to every question. We told her she would not die. She was safe. The bad, bad men were a long, long ways away and they could not harm her. When we asked her if she understood this, she said, Yes. She nodded and even smiled, like everything was clear now. Of course, of course, she was not going to die. She's only five. Everything is just beginning. This is kindergarten. Grace took Rachel's tiny hand in her own and they walked out together, mother and daughter. I lingered to talk with the school officials.

They asked when this behavior began. Did this only begin when she started school? After the attacks? They asked if anything was wrong at home. Has there been any conflict between you and your wife? Arguments? Disagreements? Fights? They asked if she was on any medication.

Perhaps she should be on some medication, the counselor said.

No, I said. She's five. I'm not putting her on drugs.

Has she ever been—abused? the teacher asked.

I looked at him.

A babysitter? he said. An uncle? A neighbor?

But I knew he was aiming closer to home.

I told him that we had told her not to talk to strangers and to tell us if anyone, even a teacher, should try to touch her in inappropriate places. We have prepared her well, I said. I tell her stories every night, stories from books and stories we make up together. We play Mozart to ease her to sleep even though it drives us, her rock 'n roll parents, crazy. We have read books on the cognitive processes of children and we seek to stimulate her mind in all the ways we can. We keep her away from the television. We have taught her to play well with others, to be kind to her fellow classmates, and to respect her peers and listen closely to her elders. But mostly we have given her a sense of the promise life holds for her, its infinite possibilities, the great adventure filled with numbers and letters and colors and green meadows and blue skies and golden sunshine.

They listened, hands in pockets, shoulders hunched. The counselor said we couldn't do much more but to let her know she was loved.

She knows that, I said. She knows that.

It was three in the morning and I was not the only one in the neighborhood who couldn't sleep. I was sitting atop the porch steps in jeans and a WMU sweatshirt, a half-empty bottle of beer in one hand and two completely empty bottles beside me, when I realized that Lester's lights were on. I knew it was three A.M., but we were all in this together, we were all Americans now, damn it, and I was just drunk enough to take the edge off. So I retrieved another two bottles of beer, figured I'd offer one to Lester, and then we'd shoot the bullshit about America and the world and how it was all going to hell in a handbasket and how everything would be different if only we were in charge.

As I crossed the gravel driveway and passed behind his truck, I realized that the blinds on the kitchen window weren't fully closed and that Lester had a guest. I smiled to myself. Lester, you old dog, you. At one end of a small table, I could see a deep red kimono and I could distinguish the shapes of a wine bottle and candles on the table. I stepped quickly and cautiously until I was standing aside the window frame, the soil beneath my feet soft and damp.

Yes! Lester said. That's exactly what he did! I couldn't believe it myself!

He laughed. Strains of soft jazz, a muted trumpet and a tenor saxophone, drifted from the living room and into the kitchen.

Tickled with excitement and curiosity, I peered through the half-open slots and was surprised when I saw that it was Lester who wore the deep red kimono.

Would you like more? Lester asked. He spoke with the same animated gestures to which I'd become accustomed, but his voice was light,
easy, free of conspiracy theories and mutual assured destruction. He
laughed again, then stood and took the bottle of wine and a near-empty
wineglass and filled the glass with a deep burgundy.

Yes, it is excellent, he said. He set the glass back on the table and
returned to his seat.

Across from Lester, there were framed photographs of a woman—in
all the pictures the same woman. She appeared much younger than
Lester.

Let me, Lester said. He half-rose in his chair and the sleeve of his
kimono caught his glass of wine. It tipped and spilled, its contents flowing to the edge of the table and down to the floor.

Shit! Fuck! Lester said. Damn it! Damn it all! Shit! Shit! Shit!

He looked around for a napkin or a towel and then realized he was
dragging the sleeve of his kimono through the spilled wine. He shook the
kimono off—he wore a white tank top and navy blue slacks beneath it—
and he crumpled the kimono in his hands and then sank back into his
chair.

I'm sorry, he said. I'm so sorry. I am so sorry.

He pushed his half-eaten plate of roast chicken, a baked potato, and
peas to the center of the table and folded his arms and lowered his head.
Before he could begin to weep, I turned on my heels and slipped back
across the driveway and into our home.

The next night, in workshop, we talked about Karl's story. Karl was a
smart-ass businessman who owned a pair of video rental stores and who
always arrived late for class, wearing a suit-and-tie, and toting a brown
bag and super-sized cola from the drive-thru at Burger King. That night
was no different. His story was based on a true story from his days growing up in inner-city Detroit in the early seventies—he was always telling
us about growing up in inner-city Detroit in the early seventies, the way
some guys are always telling you about 'Nam—and it was a sad story,
there's no way around it. Drugs and poverty and people making bad
choices and paying the price of those choices. Addiction and crack houses,

gangs and drive-by shootings. The story seemed to have a moral and the moral was this: it's society's fault, these people are victims, products of their environments. What other choices did they have?

Everyone was enthusiastically involved in the discussion, praising the gritty reality of the story, its unflinching critique of violence and institutionalized racism. Lydia, who sat in the chair closest to Dr. Louis, provided a few suggestions to make it better, ways to tighten the narrative and trim the prose. When Dr. Louis nodded in agreement and complimented her insights, self-satisfaction settled upon her face. She looked at me, only briefly, just long enough to let me know that, whatever I said, I didn't matter. I didn't belong there. Someone pointed out a problem with point of view on page three and someone else suggested a line of dialogue that seemed more realistic for the character.

When Dr. Louis realized I hadn't said a word, he asked, What do you think, Mr. Regan?

I didn't look at him. I didn't look at anybody, my ball cap pulled low to cover my eyes. I was not feeling very patriotic, not feeling very all in this together, so I told Karl to make sure the locks work. That's all. Karl, make sure the locks work.

When I returned home, I found the kitchen table covered with gas masks, rubber gloves, hunting knives, and mace. On the floor, there were containers of gasoline and kerosene and boxes of canned goods and cases of bottled water.

Where'd you get all this? I asked.

The army surplus store on Sixth Street, Grace said, a challenge in her voice. She was adjusting the straps on an industrial black gas mask. She slipped it over her head. She adjusted her blonde ponytail, and then she looked at me through the clear bug eyes of the mask. The mask had a filter that extended from where her mouth and nose should be. It made her look like a giant mouse. She shook her head from left to right and up and down, and then she removed the mask and set it on the table, apparently content with its fit.

Try that one on, she said, pointing to the table.

I didn't move.

They're Israeli, she said. Hard to get right now. Everyone's buying them. You can't even find them on the Internet.

She lifted a thin, silver case from the table, and withdrew and unfolded a knife.

Stainless steel paratrooper knife, she said. Four-and-a-half inch blade. I bought two, one for you and one for me. They're not spring-loaded so they can't accidentally open up.

She lifted a book from the table and handed it to me. I glanced at the cover. It was a survivalist handbook with a crudely drawn cover, something exploding.

Lester has a bomb shelter, she said. Did you know that? He has a bomb shelter. Underneath his house. He built it himself.

I flipped through the pages of the survivalist handbook, chapters on dressing wild game, creating poison-tipped arrows, and spending the night above the tree line in the middle of winter.

He was at the surplus store, she said. He said it's all stocked. He can go six months if he has to. He said he has room for us—if it comes to that.

It's not going to come to that, I said.

How can you be so sure?

I shook my head. Listen to yourself! I said. Do you hear what you're saying? It's not going to come to that. You're overreacting. Everyone is overreacting.

I grabbed a gas mask from the table, turned it over in my hands, and then threw it back down.

All this stuff! Jeez-us, how much did you spend on all this?

She ignored me. She lifted a box of latex gloves from the table.

For opening the mail, she said. I don't think we should open any mail that doesn't come from someone we know. I went to the pharmacy and asked about Cipro. And I want to buy a gun. I want to learn how to handle it. Shoot it. Fire it. If things go really wrong.

Things aren't going to go really wrong, I said.

I tried to reason with her. I told her the odds. We live a long way from anywhere of strategic or symbolic importance. The terrorists have never heard of this town. It's barely on the map. There are 275 million people in the United States. We spent like 60 trillion dollars on defense last year alone.

She would have none of this. I'm not going to just sit around here and wait and hope that some government official or some military general is doing everything that can be done to protect me and my family, she said. I'm not going to be helpless!

It was then that Rachel walked into the kitchen. She was wearing a gas mask, a child's gas mask, and she slipped past me to Grace, where she clutched Grace's leg with both arms.

And you wonder why our daughter acts the way she does, I said. Just look at her mother.

I turned and left the room.

But Grace wasn't finished yet. She hollered after me, At least *her mother* is trying to do something. At least *her mother* is not just sitting in front of the computer playing make-believe. She screamed that I was not doing my part, that now was the time when we must come together as a nation, as a community, and as a family to show our resolve, our character, our courage. She reminded me that I was failing, I was failing badly. I was letting the terrorists win.

I wrote a story about a black man and an old woman on a train and another story about two American soldiers in the mountains of Afghanistan. The old woman shoots the black man because she thinks he's going to take her purse and when she finds out he wasn't, she doesn't feel guilty because she figures if he didn't do it, someone else would. Better a preemptive strike. The American soldiers are hot on the trail of Osama bin Laden, but end up killing each other when they discover that one guy is sleeping with the other guy's wife.

I wrote fast, I wrote furious. I didn't bother to correct my grammatical mistakes; I didn't bother to spell-check. There's no time to spell-check when you're at war. When I turned the stories into the professor, I knew both stories had conflict and I knew the professor would make photocopies and show them to someone else, maybe a psychologist, maybe someone in charge of university security, and they'd circle my name in red ink and double-check my home address and daytime telephone number.

If they asked me about the stories, I'd deny everything. Tell them the author is dead and I'm just a messenger.

When Rachel came home the next day from school, her white tights were ripped at the knees, stained with grass and dirt, crusted black blood. Her skirt was off-kilter and her hair dangled across her face. I could see that her hands had been scraped and bloodied as well. She was sobbing as she walked toward the front door, but even from across the yard, I could tell there was a difference, an anger and a bitterness that I had not seen before. When she saw me, she suddenly stopped and dropped her backpack and stood still, sobbing, her face full of accusation. You have failed me, it said. You didn't protect me, it said. You promised, it said.

I walked across the yard to meet her and I wrapped my arms around her. She kept her own arms at her side. I lifted her and carried her inside the house, her body stiff, refusing to fold into mine. I took her to the bathroom to get her fixed up, but she refused to cooperate. She screamed at me. I want Mom, she said. I want Mom. Over and over. I want Mom.

I can do it, I said. Mom's at work.

Rachel shook her head, her arms crossed in defiance. I worried that the cuts would get infected if we waited, but I didn't want to frighten her further, so I pulled away, stepped back to the doorway, retreated to the living room.

When Grace finally arrived home, a bag of groceries in her arms, she heard Rachel in the bathroom, her voice a plaintive wail. Grace didn't bother to ask me what had happened, just handed me the bag of groceries and told me to put them away. I did. Then I stood in the doorway to the bathroom and watched as Grace attended to Rachel's wounds. They were only surface scrapes, but she winced and cried anew each time Grace touched her knee and the palms of her hands, first with a wash cloth, then with a disinfectant, and finally with a bandage. Grace offered to buy her an ice cream cone from Dairy Queen after dinner, but Rachel told Grace she didn't want to go, not for ice cream, not to school, not anywhere. Instead, she went straight to her room and closed the door.

When I asked Grace if Rachel told her what had happened, she shook her head.

Where have you been? she said. Where have you been?

The next morning I rode the bus with Rachel. I told the bus driver my little girl had been scared by all this talk of bombs and war and terrorists. The bus driver nodded in understanding—everyone understands right now, we all understand—and so I sat with Rachel in the third row on the left, aisle side, the green vinyl seats placed more closely together than I remembered.

Rachel wore a pink dress that morning. It was warm and summer still hung on. Morning light slanted through the rows of maple and elm trees that lined the streets. The bus started and stopped, kids in freshly pressed clothes climbed aboard, toting backpacks, books, lunch bags, and handheld video games. Bubble-gum pop rock played on the bus radio and the driver greeted each student by name.

Again we had bombed Afghanistan. So many days straight we didn't even bother to keep count. There were reports that Afghanistan was only the first and would not be the last. Anthrax had reached the capitol and killed a man in Florida. Violence between Israel and the Palestinians continued unabated. At ground zero, they continued to haul away crumpled steel by the ton.

When he stepped onto the bus, Rachel pointed and said, Him. I didn't hesitate. I was up from the seat and down the aisle and I had the punk kid by his shirt and I pushed him back down the steps and across the sidewalk, then shoved him to the ground, his body bent over his backpack. I pounced atop him, straddled him, shook him, then smacked him with an open palm and then cuffed him with the inside of a clenched fist. I did it again and again and again. I didn't ever want him to forget this. I told him to never, ever say something like that to a little girl, not to my little girl, not to any little girl, and the kid was screaming for me to stop but I ignored his pleas and I told him instead that if he ever did something like that again, ever so much as laid a finger upon my little girl, ever looked at my little girl, I would find him and beat the shit out of him, because she was my little girl and I would protect her from creeps like him, now and always.

I heard shouting all around me and felt hands upon my shoulders and I knew I was being pulled off him, but I kept screaming at him and kicking at him and I knew I was in deep shit now, but as they rolled me onto my stomach and pinned my arms behind my back, I looked up and saw Rachel standing at the top step of the bus. She was swinging her hips back and forth and dusting her hands together like that's that, and then I felt a boot between my shoulder blades and felt my shoulder wrenched from its socket. Still I managed to call her name—Rachel!—but her gaze was somewhere up the road, somewhere I could not see, and then a hand forced my face into the grass, into the wet, damp soil, and everything went black. It was in that moment, that brief moment between light and dark, that brief moment on a warm, autumn morning, that I finally understood: The author is dead. Long live the author.

Burn Barrel

D ixon told the dog to hold still even though he knew the dog didn't understand a single word he said. The burrs were embedded into the wet, black coat. Dixon straddled the pup and bent at the waist and held one hand on the dog's chest to calm him. With the other hand he pinched a burr between his fingernails and ripped it away. The dog barked and cross-stepped, his paws sliding on the rain-soaked boards of the porch. You get what you deserve, Dixon said. Didn't I tell you to stay out of the field and leave the rabbits alone?

The dog yelped and shook his body. Dixon grabbed the dog's collar and leaned into the dog's ear. That's enough now, hush, he said. But the dog kept barking, all jittery and skittish, and when his gaze locked onto something in the darkness beyond the yard, Dixon stopped searching for burrs. He looked up to see what had rattled the dog. The rain drummed upon the narrow bent-back road and collected and pooled in the ruts of the dirt driveway. The limbs of the willow and oak and maple trees hung heavy with the weight of precipitation. The tall grass on the far side of the road leaned toward the horizon. Beyond lay the remains of harvest, broken stalks in a late autumn cornfield.

Dixon could barely see the boy at the edge of the road but for the white horizontal stripes of his shirt.

Help me, the boy hollered. I need help.

Dixon stepped back from the dog, and when the dog raised its hackles and growled and bared his teeth, Dixon told him to shut up, but the dog ignored him. The boy entered the yard near the oak tree. His steps were unsteady and he stumbled and nearly fell against the uneven ground but he collected himself and kept moving forward. Dixon walked down the front steps in case he needed to keep the boy on neutral territory. He didn't tell the dog to stay though the dog remained on the porch, in the wash of pale light, keeping his own distance from the darkness and the boy. Dixon looked beyond the boy to the road, but he could see no one else, no car or truck, no headlights. He tried to recall if anyone drove past while he was calling the dog but he didn't remember anyone, just the rain and the barking, the rabbit scurrying into the brush and the dog's insolence. As Dixon stepped away from the porch, his eyes adjusted to the darkness. He could see the boy better, each cautious as they neared one another.

Promise me you won't call the cops, the boy said. Promise me that. Can you promise me?

The boy bled from the forehead and the nose and blood ran over his cheeks and stained his rugby shirt. His clothes were soaked from the rain—the shirt, his blue jeans, his white tennis shoes. His blonde hair lay matted against his skull.

Dixon stopped and squared his shoulders. He braced himself, the rain sharp in his face.

What do you want? Dixon asked.

The boy stood a few feet from Dixon, and his body shook with the chill. Dixon could see that the boy was crying, the wetness wasn't all rain.

You have to promise me, the boy said. You can't call the cops.

The boy was rail-thin, maybe sixteen, and the clothes seemed too big for his frame. Dixon wondered if the boy was drunk or high and had he killed someone or had someone tried to kill the boy. The boy held out his hands with the palms upward, the rain collecting there too, washing away the small streaks of blood.

He was fucking her, the boy said. He was fucking her.

The dog brushed against Dixon's leg and a bolt of adrenaline shot through his body and then he looked down and saw the dog, its black coat barely visible in the darkness.

Why doesn't anybody love me? the boy said.

Dixon thought it was a stupid thing to say, but then the boy's shoulders convulsed and he stood in the rain and he cried. So Dixon did not leave the boy, instead he waited although the boy's question alone did not explain why he stood in Dixon's yard.

Why don't we get you inside, get you out of the rain, Dixon said, his voice cautious and measured.

If you can't promise, maybe I should just keep going, the boy protested. I won't hold it against you. But Dixon said, You can't stay out here, not like this. We need to get you cleaned up.

He turned his shoulders to indicate to the boy that they should go inside, but Dixon did not turn all the way around. He kept his eye on the boy.

Do you promise not to call the cops? the boy asked. Because I'm in deep shit.

I promise, Dixon said, though he knew promises didn't mean anything in a moment like this and he knew the boy should not take him at his word because he would not take the boy's word.

The dog growled and barked but Dixon did not tell him to hush, just took him by his collar and held him still. Dixon told the boy again to go on inside and the boy hesitated, then walked up the steps to the porch and opened the door and stepped inside. Dixon snapped the leash on the dog's collar and followed the boy into the house, never taking his eyes from the boy's hands, even as he told the dog to sit and to stay and finally pushed the dog away to close the door.

The boy stood in the entryway, water dripping from his clothes and pooling around his shoes on the hardwood floor. Dixon hung his barn coat on the wall and began to tell the boy to take off his shoes, but then changed his mind and pointed down the narrow hallway that divided the house into two halves. On your left, he said.

The boy moved down the hallway, the rubber soles of his shoes squeaking against the floor. When he reached the door to the bathroom, he hesitated, and Dixon stepped past him and reached inside and flicked on the light. The boy stepped into the room and shielded his eyes against the bright artificial light. Dixon followed with a pair of washcloths and hand towels from the adjacent linen closet. The boy stood in front of the mirror over the sink and for the first time saw what Dixon had already seen.

Oh my God, the boy said. Look at me.

And he began to cry again.

The boy's forehead looked as though someone had run a cheese grater across it, the skin torn and sliced and embedded with small shards of glass. The nose was swollen and clotted with blood, a darker shade of red than streaked his forehead. A knot had formed above his right eyebrow.

Dixon ran hot water from the faucet and took a washcloth and held it under the steaming water, then squeezed the excess water from it and lifted it to the boy's forehead. He tried to touch it gently, but the boy winced, then screamed, and Dixon abruptly pulled back, squeezing the wet cloth in his fist, water splashing on the floor.

I can do that, the boy said, and he took the wet cloth from Dixon's hand and gently daubed it against his forehead.

Dixon watched the boy and the boy watched himself in the mirror as he picked little pieces of glass from his forehead.

Wait, Dixon said.

He took hold of the boy's right arm and lowered it and turned it over, palm down. A jagged cut ran from the back of the boy's thumb to the far side of his wrist. The water had washed away the initial clotting and it bled freely again. Dixon wiped the washcloth across the cut to clean it. The boy bit his lip and closed his eyes. Dixon told him to hold the wet cloth in place and opened the medicine cabinet above the sink. He took out an antibiotic ointment, a box of gauze and a spool of white medical tape.

Hold your hand out, he said.

I'm so sorry, the boy said. I am so sorry. I shouldn't even be here. This is so fucked up.

It's okay, Dixon said.

No it's not, the boy said. Everything is wrong. Everything.

The boy's hand shook as Dixon covered it with gauze and wrapped the tape around the boy's thumb and wrist, the blood quickly soaking through the gauze. The boy choked as he tried to speak.

Do you know what it's like, the boy asked, to be fucked over by the person you love, the person you love the most in the whole goddamned world?

Dixon didn't reply. He rinsed the cloth under the hot water and gave it back to the boy. The boy took the cloth in his left hand and touched it to his forehead, fresh blood filling the cuts when he pulled the cloth away again.

He was in bed with her, the boy said. He was fucking her! And I come home from work and I find them in bed together. And they don't even care! I said, Ryan, what's going on, and he told me to pack up my shit and get the hell out! Out of my place! He told me to get the fuck out. They didn't even care! They were laughing at me!

He dabbed the cloth against the knot above his eye.

How does someone do that to you? the boy asked.

He leaned his head back to examine his nose. Is it broken? he asked.

Dixon leaned forward. Tilt your head back down, he said.

The boy did.

I don't think so. But I can't tell.

Oh fuck, the boy said. What am I going to do? Look at this.

The boy leaned against the sink and placed the cloth underneath the stream of hot water again, washed the blood from it, then squeezed it and brought it back to his forehead.

So I left, he said. I just left. I took my car and I drove around for awhile trying to figure out what to do. I didn't know what else to do, I didn't have no place else to go and I didn't care anymore and I know I'm this total fuck-up, I really am, believe me. Then I saw this telephone poll and I knew what I was going to do. I went as fast as I could and I went straight at it, just floored it. But I couldn't even do that right. Fuck.

The boy winced and held his hand open to reveal a small chip of glass.

It's always been this way, he said. Every time I trust someone. I just get walked all over. It's like I have a sign. Step on me. Fuck me. I mean, Ryan is the first person who I thought really cared about me. About me. Me. Me me me. And Sarah? She was supposed to be my best friend. They were fucking. In my bed! He told me he didn't even think about women and he was fucking her the whole damn time.

Dixon looked at the kid again. What did you say? he asked.

The boy looked at him. My boyfriend was fucking her the whole time, he said.

Dixon nodded. Oh. Okay. I see.

What?

Dixon shook his head. The glass. In your forehead. You hit the windshield.

No shit, the boy said.

And then he started to cry again.

Dixon watched the boy wipe the blood from his forehead and his nose and rinse the washcloth in the white ceramic sink, the blood mixing with the water and curling around the bowl before sliding down the drain. The boy opened his mouth and everything poured out: the father who left when the boy was two weeks old; the endless string of his mother's boyfriends; and the boyfriend who gave her an ultimatum when the boy was thirteen, said it was either him or the boy, one of them had to go. His mother told the boy to get out and so he did, didn't even pack his clothes. Dixon gave him the ointment from the medicine cabinet and watched him unscrew the cap and squeeze the tube and lay a tubular strip of cream across his finger. He winced at the sting of the antibiotic as he pressed it against the dozens of tiny cuts. The boy told him how he'd lived on the streets in Atlanta and Memphis until his grandparents tracked him down and took him in. He'd stayed with them in Lansing until they found out he was doing ecstasy and smoking pot and occasionally crack, and they'd kicked him out, afraid he'd get caught and they'd get arrested. Dixon examined the boy's face and neck and hands for signs, for marks, for open sores and lesions. He saw the pimples and the acne scars and a purple bruise behind the ear and a pinkish scar just below the line of his jaw. Dixon wondered if he'd know it if he saw it, saw it right in front of his own eyes beneath the bright lights of his own bathroom. He saw the crusted blood on the boy's collar and his ear and in the sink and on the washcloth from the linen closet and drops on the tile floor. He wondered what the boy had already touched and if he had surgical gloves somewhere in the house, maybe beneath the kitchen sink with the cleaning supplies. He wondered what the boy would say if he put them on. Everything welled up out of the boy, and Dixon tried not to sound trite when he told the boy everything would be okay, things would get better. When the boy covered his face with his hands, Dixon looked down into the open palms of his own hands to check for cuts, even a small one from the briars or the burrs or from working on the roof the past weekend, but the boy pulled his hands away and opened his eyes again before Dixon could be sure. He closed his hands and looked at the boy. The boy asked him to re-bandage his hand. The gauze had become soaked with water.

I need to get out of these clothes, the boy said. They're so wet.

Okay, Dixon said. Okay.

Look at me. I'm shivering like a wet hen.

Dixon backed toward the doorway. I'll get you something dry to wear, he said. You do the bandage. You can do that, can't you? I'll only be a second.

The boy nodded. Dixon went upstairs to his bedroom and opened the door and flicked on the light. He pulled open a dresser drawer and withdrew a plain white T-shirt and closed the drawer. He opened a second drawer and from the bottom of a pile removed a faded, black cotton sweatshirt. He held it up and let it unfold in front of him. He knew it would be too big for the boy and he thought of Carter's clothes, they would've been a much better fit, but Dixon knew he'd thrown those out too when Lila had left for Texas and taken his son with her.

When Dixon returned downstairs, he found the boy in the living room, his forehead streaked with white cream. The fireplace lay dormant and the furniture was thick and sturdy. The walls were bare but for a pair of framed photographs—a wheat field in summer, full-bodied and golden with a bright blue sky, and what appeared to be the same field in winter, snow-swept and gray.

You live alone? the boy asked.

Dixon nodded.

Not married?

Dixon shook his head. He handed the boy the T-shirt and the sweatshirt and the boy set the clothes on a glass-topped coffee table next to a pile of magazines. Metal paperclips marked a handful of pages. One magazine was open, face down. Beside it a sketch pad and a set of colored pencils.

What's this? the boy asked. He leaned over and turned the sketch pad so that he could read the scribbled markings.

Nothing, Dixon said.

The boy lifted the magazine from the table. It was a home redecorating magazine. The boy examined the open pages—on the left, a brightly lit child's bedroom with a set of bunk beds, a wooden toy box, shelves with stuffed animals, a soapbox car trophy and hardback books; on the right, the same room converted into an office with a drafting table, track lighting, a pair of framed Van Gogh prints, and a high-quality stereo system.

Could you put that down, please? Dixon said.

The boy apologized and did as Dixon asked. He set the magazine down, careful not to crease the pages.

I should go, the boy said.

There's no hurry, Dixon said, trying to reassure the boy. He feared what the boy might do, how close to the edge he might still stand. Dixon gestured with a small wave of his hand toward the dry clothes on the table. See how they fit, he said.

Dixon stepped back to allow the boy an unobstructed path to the privacy of the bathroom. Instead, with his one good hand, the boy stood in the center of the living room and drew the wet and bloody rugby shirt over his head. Dixon saw the thin, bony upper torso made bare. The boy's ribs were visible and his skin was pale and ghostly white and smooth with small pink nipples. Dixon thought the wind would crush the boy's chest. The boy's jeans sagged on his hips and hung beneath the gray elastic waistband of his blue boxer shorts. It seemed impossible that they didn't fall to his ankles. For a moment, Dixon nearly told the boy he should wear a belt, but then he heard Lila's voice in his head, telling him to let other people live their own lives.

The boy dropped the rugby shirt to the floor and looked to Dixon. Dixon raised his eyes from the boy's body to the boy's eyes.

You can look, the boy said. It doesn't bother me.

You need a towel, Dixon said. I'll get you a towel.

Dixon turned and left the living room and walked down the hallway to the linen closet. When he returned a moment later, the boy was still bare-chested and the dog was barking and clawing against the front door, encouraged by the sound of voices and footsteps. Dixon gave the towel to the boy.

What's with the dog? the boy asked.

Dixon eyed the door as though he could see the dog outside on the porch. He's just a pup, barely a year old, Dixon said, glad to speak of anything else. But spoiled. Got used to being inside and living a life of luxury. Now that he has to fend for himself outside he's always getting himself into trouble. Ain't smart enough for his own good sometimes, like tonight, chasing a damn rabbit into the brush where he knows he's gonna get all snagged up in the barbs and the briars. He does it anyway, then comes howling to me so I can pick 'em off.

The boy opened the towel and wiped it over his chest, raising his thin, stalk-like arms.

He seems like an okay dog, the boy said.

You want him? Dixon asked.

I can't take care of myself. The boy smiled. Why would I wanna take care of a damn dog?

Dixon nodded. The boy wrapped the towel around his shoulders to dry his back and then he picked the rugby shirt off the floor and handed it and the towel back to Dixon. Dixon held both items away from his body. He looked around the room for someplace to put them. Finally he carried them back to the bathroom and dropped them on the floor. He wiped his hands on a fresh towel, then quickly scrubbed his hands with soap and hot water before drying them again and dropping that towel too atop the pile of wet clothes. When he returned to the living room, he asked the boy if he wanted something to drink.

Coffee? Hot chocolate? Tea?

You got something harder?

The boy brushed his hands down the T-shirt to smooth out the wrinkles. It hung well off his shoulders and nearly down to mid-thigh. Dixon began to tell the boy he didn't have any whiskey and besides a boy his age shouldn't be drinking hard liquor, all it did to a young body. But he fought the urge to lecture—this was a lesson he needed to learn, isn't that what she had said?

Haven't I seen you someplace before? the boy asked. In town maybe?

I don't think so.

Yeah, I have. I know I have. I've seen you at the lumberyard. You work for Ellis?

Do you know Ellis?

I hate Ellis, that son of a bitch. But I'm friends with Teddy. You know Teddy? Looks just like old man Ellis except no beard. Just that baby face.

Dixon nodded. Used to sort of, he said. He and my son were friends.

When they were younger.

Where's your son now?

With his mother. In Texas.

What are they doing in Texas? Long way from here to Texas.

Dixon shrugged. I don't know. That's just where they live. I have no idea what people do in Texas.

You divorced?

More or less.

The boy laughed. Dixon was shocked by the sound, its sharp retort. You don't sound like you know what you're talking about, the boy said.

I'm not sure I do.

The boy slid the sweatshirt over his arms and gripped the hole for his head and held it stretched open.

You got a name? Dixon asked.

Not one that matters, the boy said. He pulled the sweatshirt over his head and left it and the T-shirt untucked, everything far too big for his body.

Dixon and the boy stood in the kitchen. The boy drank whiskey on the rocks from a cut-glass tumbler and Dixon drank hot tea from a ceramic coffee mug. The rain drummed against the roof, and the door on the utility shed repeatedly slammed open and shut. Dixon would've gone and locked it but he didn't want to leave the boy alone in the house. The whiskey calmed the boy, warmed his veins, and he leaned back against the counter and acted as though nothing was out of the ordinary tonight, just two men who had met in the course of the day and were unwinding over drinks in the kitchen.

What do you do? the boy asked.

Work.

Well, yeah, but where?

Here and there.

You like it out here?

Well enough.

Quiet?

Yeah.

I could get used to this, the boy said. Being way out here. At first I thought I'd be walking all night, no houses anywhere. Then I seen your lights.

Dixon cupped his hands around the mug. He looked around the kitchen for something to talk about. The floor tiles had been scrubbed clean and bright. The single set of dishes from dinner had been washed and put away. The shelves behind the cupboard doors held neatly ordered rows of canned goods and boxed pasta. Burnished copper pots and pans hung from hooks above the stove.

It's a nice place.

Thank you.

You can tell you've worked hard on it, ain't you?

Dixon nodded.

Everything's like in the perfect place.

I like it that way, Dixon said.

Dixon added a teaspoon of sugar to his tea, stirred it with a spoon. The boy poured himself more whiskey.

Why don't you got any pictures of your wife and kid around? the boy asked.

I just don't.

They got 'em all?

You could say that.

Why'd they leave? the boy asked.

Dixon glared at the boy. You ask a lot of questions, he said.

Only way to get answers.

Dixon nodded. He didn't like the boy's attitude, his new-found confidence. Cockiness. That's what it was. What all these kids had. He decided to ignore the boy's question. Why'd they leave? Who could know? The boy should ask Lila. She was the one who'd left. He was done with that now. Should've been done with that a long time ago. It had been Lila who'd wanted to make things complicated, who kept demanding more from him. He'd tried. But they were gone now.

Finish your whiskey, Dixon told the boy. It was good whiskey and it shouldn't go to waste.

When the boy had finished his second glass of whiskey, he asked if he could make a long-distance phone call. My mother lives in Florida, he said. Maybe I can go stay with her. I'll pay you back. I promise.

The phone's in the hallway, near the foot of the stairs, Dixon said. You don't have to pay me back.

Dixon followed the boy down the hallway, a fresh mug of tea in hand. The boy took the handset from its cradle on the small wooden table and punched in a series of digits. Dixon leaned against the wall as the boy waited for an answer.

Finally, the boy said, It's me. Your son. Remember me? Yeah. I'm still here.

Dixon turned and walked back down the hallway toward the kitchen. He wanted to respect the boy's privacy. The boy took another drink of his whiskey, the ice rattling inside the glass.

Pick up the phone, he said. Pick up the goddamned phone. I know you're there.

Dixon walked across the kitchen and dumped his cup of tea into the sink and washed out the mug. He could still hear the boy.

You bitch. I fucking hate you. I've always hated you.

Dixon capped the bottle of whiskey and placed it on the counter. He thought, That's no way to talk to your mother, but he left the boy alone. This wasn't his problem. It was between the boy and his mother. What did Dixon know about raising a son anyway? Isn't that what Lila had said?

Goddamn you, you bitch, you fucking whore.

There was a long silence and then Dixon heard the click of the handset in its cradle. A few moments later the boy appeared again in the doorway to the kitchen, his face pinched and crimson with anger.

I'm fucked, he said.

Maybe she just wasn't home.

It's a weeknight.

Dixon returned to the table and sat quietly, folding and unfolding his hands in front of him.

But thanks, the boy said. Thanks for trying. I appreciate it. I really do.

Is there anyone else you could call? Dixon asked.

The boy laughed, again that sharp retort, like a rifle blast.

Dixon tried to think of someone else who might love the boy, but he could think of no one. The boy set his glass on the table.

Listen, he said. It's late. I'm going to get out of here. Move along.

No, Dixon said, you don't have to . . .

But the boy cut him off. I'm imposing, as they say, and you probably have work in the morning. I should go. I've been a burden.

Dixon didn't try to argue. He rose from his chair at the kitchen table and followed the boy into and down the hallway until they stood in the entryway by the front door. The dog heard the footsteps and started to bark again. Dixon hollered for him to hush.

Aw, man, the boy said. These clothes. I can't take these clothes.

Dixon shook his head. Don't worry about it. You can't wear that other shirt. It's soaking wet. Blood-soaked, too, Dixon thought, though he did not say it.

Thanks. Thank you.

Where you gonna go? Dixon asked.

I don't know, the boy said. I don't know. I'll figure something out.

There was an awkward pause, the boy's good hand on the doorknob, Dixon's hands in his jeans pockets.

Look, Dixon said, why don't you let me take you to the hospital, let someone take a look at those cuts?

The boy looked Dixon in the eye and Dixon thought the boy would start to cry again. He shook his head. No, no, no. You promised.

Dixon raised his hands, palms open to show the boy he meant no harm.

Here, Dixon said. He stepped quickly to the small table near the steps where the phone rested. He took a pen and a slip of paper and he wrote his phone number on the slip and gave it to the boy.

You need anything, you call me, he said. I don't want you killing yourself tonight.

Dixon smiled at the boy to let him know it was a lighthearted joke, the kind of joke they could exchange now at this late hour because the boy wouldn't kill himself now, right? Not after all this.

The boy thanked him and put the slip of paper in his pocket.

It's like you're an angel or something, the boy said.

No it's not.

Yes it is. It's like you saved me.

Dixon looked away from the boy. He couldn't bear to see the boy's dark eyes or the too big black sweatshirt or the torn skin of his forehead or the purple and yellow of bruise that was spreading across his nose and around his eyes. When he looked away, the boy stepped forward and placed a hand on Dixon's upper arm and his lips on Dixon's cheek. Then the boy pulled away and opened the door and closed it behind him and hurried past the dog, which raised up and barked and growled and then lay back down on the porch as the boy disappeared into the darkness and the rain.

Dixon held his hands and a fresh washcloth beneath the hot water in the bathroom sink for as long as he could, until his skin turned pink and red and he could bear the pain no longer. The steam rose from the sink and clouded the mirror and he scrubbed his cheek with the washcloth until he thought the skin would bleed and then he washed his hands again and his arms. From beneath the kitchen sink, he removed his cleaning supplies, and when he returned to the bathroom, he wore black rubber gloves and sprinkled disinfectant over the sink and the bathroom tiles and got down on his hands and knees and scrubbed and rinsed until all the drops of blood were gone. He disinfected the kitchen counter and the table and the phone and the hallway table upon which the phone sat. He placed the towels and the washcloths into a black plastic trash bag and the boy's rugby shirt, too, heavy with water, and he retrieved the glass from which the boy had drunk his whiskey, the whiskey gone, the ice melted, and he dropped it into the trash bag as well.

He carried the bag through the house and out the backdoor and across the yard, past the clothesline and the garden and the utility shed to the burn barrel. It was a thick blackness behind the house, no moon, no stars, everything hidden by the storm clouds. From the front of the house he heard the dog barking into the darkness and scrambling from one end of the porch to the other, his paws sliding on the wet boards. Dixon removed the rusted metal cover from the barrel and dropped the trash bag inside. He went back inside and returned with a pile of newspapers and a small glass container of kerosene. He dropped the newspapers into the barrel and doused the pile in kerosene, then returned inside for matches. It only took one for the kerosene to light and the newspapers to erupt in flame. When Dixon was certain the fire would hold, he set the top of the burn barrel in place, leaving enough space for oxygen to feed the flames. Then Dixon looked to the sky and prayed that the rain wouldn't snuff it out.

Inside the house, Dixon called the police. He told them about the boy and the car and the telephone pole. Told them he'd last seen the boy on Farrand Road and he described the sweatshirt he'd given the boy and his blue jeans and tennis shoes and his matted blond hair. The officer said they'd been looking all over for the driver, it wasn't even the boy's car, he'd stolen it from his roommate, and if he was alive, he was lucky to be alive. Dixon said he just wanted to make sure the boy was going to be all right. He told the officer the boy had been hysterical and suicidal at first, at least that's how he acted. The officer thanked him for his time and then he hung up. He didn't even ask for Dixon's telephone number. Nor did Dixon get to tell him everything he had to say. About the boy. About Lila. About his own son. About promises made and broken.

The phone rang. Dixon looked at the clock. It was nearly quarter to four. He slipped out of bed and hurried to the head of the stairs, the hardwood floor cold on his bare feet. And then he stopped, his heart pounding with the adrenaline that comes with the ring of the phone in the middle of the night. The phone rang four times and then the answering machine clicked and the boy's voice came over the speaker.

Hey. It's me, he said. Are you there?

The boy paused. Dixon could hear the answering machine's tape as it wound itself from one spool to the other.

I need a place to stay tonight. I don't got nowhere to go. And I was thinking maybe I could stay with you.

Dixon waited.

It's cold out here, you know. And wet. Not a good night for camping, huh.

Dixon held his ground.

I guess you're not there or maybe you're sleeping and so maybe you won't hear this 'til morning. Or maybe you just figure you're done with me. But I guess I should say thank you anyway.

There was a long silence and then the boy hung up and Dixon heard the click, and the tape on the answering machine stopped rolling.

The phone rang. The machine clicked. The boy's voice.

Pick up the goddamn phone. I know you're there. I know you're fucking there. I need some help here. I need you, damn it. Please. Please. Please pick up the phone.

Dixon looked at the clock. Not fifteen minutes had passed. They both waited.

I know you're there.

The tape stopped.

Dixon walked downstairs. He turned off the answering machine and shut off the ringer on the phone. He walked to the front door and he unlocked it and opened it. The dog looked up at him in the frame of the doorway. Dixon reached down and unhooked the chain from the dog's collar and the dog followed him inside.

Dixon closed the door and locked and dead-bolted it. He double-checked the backdoor to make sure it was dead-bolted too and then he went to the linen closet and found a towel and called the dog to him. The dog came and stood patiently before him as Dixon wiped the wet, black coat with the towel. He found another burr and pulled it free and then a second and when he was convinced there were no more, he hung the towel over the banister and shut off the light. Upstairs, in his bedroom, Dixon slipped beneath the covers again and pulled them over his chest. The dog waited until Dixon had stopped moving and then placed his front paws on the edge of the bed and jumped up and lay atop the covers.

Outside it was quiet and still. The front had moved past and the sky behind it had begun to clear. The fire in the burn barrel had reduced everything to ash and burned itself out. Soon the dog fell asleep, its flanks rising and falling in rhythm with its breathing. Dixon lay on his back and stared into the ceiling and wondered if his dog dreamed about Texas, and he waited for the morning to come.

Be a Missionary

I always felt sorry for the missionaries. To live along the Amazon in the dense foliage of the rain forest, a two days' journey by boat to the nearest mail station or toilet paper or color TV. Or to live on the barren plains of Niger, dinner a paste made from grain crushed in stone bowls and mixed with goat's milk, daily laundry in the fecal brown river. Always there were the notes in their mimeographed letters about political instability and the threat of a violent insurrection to be led by a Marxist one summer, a *Generalissimo* in the winter, a puppet republican in the spring. There was the eleven-hour drive to the capitol for a necessary signature and the sign on the door that said, "Come back tomorrow." The tribal chief who wanted you to leave by sundown or he'd personally cut out your heart. Malaria and dysentery and piranhas and viruses unknown to Western doctors, untreatable with Western cures. Pythons and boiled monkey's brains and the vast dark spaces of the earth untouched by electricity or God's grace. And then this: furlough. A year or six months back in the United States after four years abroad. An overloaded Chrysler station wagon with 160,000 miles, bald tires, no air conditioning, and an overheated radiator. Secondhand clothes, migraines, and heartburn. The children bickering in the back seat. Two-lane roads, illegible directions, gas station bathrooms, a pay phone, and finally a sullen congregation of forty on a summer Sunday evening in my father's church.

But Rod Rudd didn't want us to feel sorry for him. He wanted us to be excited, to be on fire for the Lord, to see the field before us ripe for the harvest. He was ex-military, a former Air Force pilot who had flown fifty missions in Vietnam, but now he was on a different mission, a mission from God, a mission to spread the good news of Jesus Christ, of His death, burial, and resurrection. "One day He's coming again and that day will be soon," Rod assured us.

Rod Rudd paused at the edge of the stage and leaned out over the congregation. I was seated in the front row with my brothers, my sisters, and my parents. I was ten years old. I instinctively leaned back, cautious of being caught in the sweep of Rod Rudd's sway. He told us he had a heart for people and for the suffering of this life—for the oppression of sin, for the oppression of poverty and disease, for the oppression of dictators and godless communists. He still wore a buzz cut, gone a bit gray now, and though his belly was paunchier than it must have been fifteen years before, his face still had the lean features of a bare-fisted fighter and his hands were long and thick, the sort of hands you imagine could strangle a charging camel by the neck. He talked fast, everything a rush, a blur of words he could barely contain. He quoted verses of scripture by the dozens, smiled and joked and prowled the stage unrestrained by pulpit or altar. He thanked my father for the opportunity to be here this evening and he thanked the congregation for its graciousness and its continued support through prayer and generous financial contributions.

Rod Rudd was married with three children. His wife—"Stand up, Carolyn"—sat with their three children on the other side of the auditorium. One by one, as they were introduced by Rod, they stood and turned to the congregation and nodded—"James is our oldest, he's fourteen, a bona fide chip off the old block. Sara, she's eleven, a firecracker and she's gonna be a heartbreaker. Luke, only seven, but a handful already." The boys wore plaid sport coats and ties and Sara wore a peasant dress nearly identical to her mother's. Later they would sing an *a cappella* version of "What a Friend We Have in Jesus."

To listen to Rod Rudd was to listen to a modern-day Paul, a man in the world, but not of the world, once a man of the sword, now a man of the Word. He was a regular fundamentalist Renaissance man, a scholar of the Bible, a molder of men, an airplane pilot, and a repairer of all mechanical things great and small. He described the landing of his seaplane on a narrow stretch of river in the middle of a torrential equatorial downpour, the pregnant mother in the back seat about to give birth, the

plane whipping back and forth in the gale-force winds, his wife waiting
on the banks below to deliver the child, a nephew of the tribal chief.

"Thank God," he said. "Praise Jesus."

But the congregation had heard it all before. (Show the slides! I
thought. Just show the slides! I want to look at the pictures.) The testi-
monies all sounded the same. "We met at Bible college. . . ." "We had no
idea that He would send us to _____." "Last year alone we saw
_____ people come to know Christ as their personal Lord and Savior.
. . ." "This past year we dedicated our new church building, though it's
just cement blocks with a thatch roof." (Show the slides! Show the slides!
Dad, can I get the lights?)

No one mentioned money, but it was the unspoken purpose of the
visit. This was not just a lesson in world geography. The missionaries
needed to raise the support necessary to enable them to spend four years
bringing light to the darkness, to go places the rest of us would never go.
To raise support was another way of saying they needed to beg for money.
Ten dollars a month? Twenty dollars a month? Five dollars a month? "If
you can't give financially, you can support us with your prayers. Sign up
on the prayer warrior sheet in the back and we'll send you our monthly
newsletter." (Last year's highlights included Mrs. Rudd's bout with
eczema, the boys' introduction to botany and fractions, and the incident
with the witch doctor's bicycle.)

The windows were open. The missionary prayer cards functioned as
primitive fans. Across the aisle, Mrs. Davidson filed her nails and the
Benson kids were drawing spaceships in the back of the hymnals. Even
my father couldn't hide his boredom.

My mother stared out the window. Rod Rudd was my mother's ex-
boyfriend. I didn't know this. Not yet. But I would.

I admit my attention had been drifting when Rod Rudd began to tell the
story. There had been a trip to a nearby village and rain, heavy rains and
floods, washed-out bridges, a suggestion that the family spend the night
in the village. But Carolyn needed to be back to assist the local medical
team with a prenatal workshop. So they piled into the truck, an old
Chevy that belonged to the mission, one of those clunkers that had been

overhauled a hundred times now, and they started out on the way. Rod was driving and it was getting dark and it was pouring rain, torrents of rain, and the wipers just couldn't go back and forth fast enough. The windows steamed up and Rod drove slow, the tires slipping back and forth on the muddy dirt road. His biggest concern was getting bogged down in the mud and having to get out and push.

"And maybe that's what I was thinking about—about not wanting to get any wetter than we already were," Rod said, "about getting mud on my pants and my jacket—and so I didn't see the dog until we hit it and there was the noise of the impact and the force of the impact.

"I panicked," Rod said, "I can admit that. I swung the wheel and lost control, the tires skidding and the truck turning sideways and we could feel the truck leaving the road—it felt like we went airborne though they never could determine for certain—and when we finally stop slipping and sliding—a great breaking of glass and crunch of metal—I look up and there's a metal post through the center of my son's chest."

From the front row, I locked my eyes on Rod Rudd. I couldn't take them off him. Not now.

"It's there," Rod said. "Right there in front of me. I reach out and touch it. I'm sure he's dead. I'm sure I've killed my son. I'm touching the metal post and it's cold and it's wet and I'm trying to figure out where it came from. And then James opens his eyes and looks at me—just looks at me, not like anything special, not like he knows anything is wrong—he just looks at me.

"Carolyn is on the other side of him, closest to the door, and she sees what I see and she starts to cry, to weep, and I don't know what to do. I mean, what can I do? There's a metal post through my son's chest. And then Sara—she's in back still, her and Luke—she starts to pray. Her little voice from the back of the truck. I can still hear her voice.

"So I say, 'Sara, you okay? Luke?' And they both say, 'Yeah, okay. What happened?' And I say, 'We had an accident.' Said it like it was the simplest, most obvious thing in the world. I'm trying not to panic, you know.

"James says, 'Take it out, Dad. It hurts.' I don't know what to say or what to do. But I decide I have to do what he asks. So I wrap my fingers around the metal post—and I realize now it's a fence post, something used for barbed wire or something like that and it's old and there are rust spots on it and my mind is thinking that my son is going to die, this is how he will die. 'Take it out, Dad. It hurts.' That's what he said. And so I wrap my hands around it and as gently as I can I start to pull. Nothing happens. So I start to pray too. Just say, 'Lord, this is up to you. My son is your son. If you want him, take him. But take him quickly and painlessly. But, Lord, if you would, please let him stay with us.' And I pull. And I pull. And I feel the pole start to slide back out and I close my eyes—I couldn't watch, I couldn't bear the sight of all the blood that was flowing down my son's chest and I could hear him fighting to breathe, to get air into his lungs, and I thought, 'My God, it's punctured his lungs, it's punctured his heart.'

"I don't know how long the pole was. I pulled it out—it seemed to keep coming forever and my hands were wet from the rain and wet now from his warm blood—and I tossed it back through the shattered windshield. And then we huddled there in the front seat, trying to stay warm against the wet, cold rain. Me, James, Carolyn, Sara, and Luke. And God."

Rod Rudd paused and I could the hear whoop-whoop-whoop of the ceiling fans and the slight buzz of the p.a. system. From behind us, a cough, apologetic even in its interruption. Rod Rudd stood with one button of his sport coat still buttoned, his hands in his pants pockets. He was sweating in the summer heat, sweating beneath the lights in the small auditorium.

"The hour is getting late," Rod Rudd said, "and it's a long story that brings us to stand before you tonight. God is good. God is so good. By all rights, James shouldn't be with us here tonight. He should be dead. The doctors say it's a miracle. That the metal pole went right through his heart and back out the other side. A metal pole. Right through the center of his heart. Yet there is he. As alive as you and me."

By now everything was silent. Across the auditorium eyes turned to the family and the miracle boy seated there. They sat together dutifully in the third row, eyes straight ahead. Rod gestured in the direction of the boy. "Come on up," he said.

A gangly boy with straight blond hair and a slumped frame stood. He obediently slipped past his mother and his siblings and into the outside aisle. He walked past the organ and took the two steps onto the stage with the grace of a bird.

He turned to face the congregation and gave a sheepish smile and a small half-wave of his hand. Then he loosened his tie and lifted his collar and pulled the noose of the tie up and over his head. As he unbuttoned the shirt, working downward, pulling the shirttails out from his belted slacks, Rod said, "You have to excuse us here, but I want you to see the miracle."

When the shirt was fully unbuttoned, James pulled it off and then he raised a white T-shirt over his head and stood there, bare-chested, the T-shirt in hand. His father didn't need to point, didn't need to show where the metal pole had impaled the boy's body—we could see the ragged, ugly red scar right over where his heart must be. It was neither small nor neat nor insignificant. It spoke of violence and violation. It was not a surgeon's scar, it was the scar of a javelin hurled through flesh and bone, ripping and tearing indiscriminately.

"Turn around," Rod Rudd said.

James turned around.

On his back, there was another jagged red scar, directly opposite.

The boy turned around again.

"He oughta be dead," Rod Rudd said. "Every doctor in every city we've been to says he oughta be dead. That there's no way on God's green earth that my boy should be alive today. But I'm telling you this. It's exactly because this is God's green earth that my boy is alive today. Amen? He who holds the future in the palm of His hand holds each of us. Nothing can harm a hair on our heads unless He says it may. And He declared that it was not yet time for my boy to die. Not yet time. Not yet time. And I believe that God has great things ahead for my boy."

Rod Rudd nodded to his son and the boy pulled the T-shirt back over his head and stepped off the stage. I watched him as he sat beside his mother and finished putting his shirt back on, buttoning it up and pulling the tie back into place. I thought he was the luckiest boy on the face of the earth.

We were always the last ones to leave, my father lingering to shut off the lights and lock up the doors. That night was no different. We helped the Rudds take down their display table, to pack away the photos and the totems and the map of Brazil and the World Book Encyclopedia Factoids that tried to bring that faraway place a little bit closer to the people and the churches they visited.

The congregation had cleared out quickly. It was summer and there was still another hour or two of daylight, time to sit on the porch and drink lemonade, to listen to the sound of televisions and family conversations through the open windows and screen doors of the neighborhood.

Rod and my father talked about baseball as they carried the boxes to the station wagon, and Carolyn and my mother picked through the missionary supply table at the back of the foyer, my mother checking items off a list as Carolyn chose: paper towels, notebooks, homemade pot holders, boxes of pasta, a pair of sewing needles, a dozen copies of the Wordless Book—items they could use in Brazil. Outside, the Rudd children sat together on the edge of the sidewalk, picking grass from the church lawn. It was late summer and the lawn was still lush enough that I had to help my father mow the lawn every Saturday morning. James had a soccer ball between his feet. My brothers and sisters were chasing lightning bugs, Esther squealing each time Nathan opened his hand and threw a gold-lit bug in her direction.

I wandered into my father's study and browsed the shelves of books that lined the walls. There were thousands of books. The most impressive were the sets of biblical commentaries, thick, hardback tomes that glossed and exegeted every chapter and verse in the Bible. They seemed as though they belonged in a library, ancient texts stamped with gold-leaf. There were bible dictionaries and concordances and atlases, Greek and Hebrew lexicons, books on apologetics and Israel and prophecy and dispensationalism, study guides to the writings of Paul, the Gospels, the Pentateuch, books on church history with handwritten notes in the margin, Spire paperbacks on the demons of rock 'n roll and marijuana, a copy of the Book of Mormon, a Catholic Bible with the Apocrypha. On the wall hung his two framed degrees, one from the college and one from the seminary. A gray, metallic, four-drawer file cabinet contained his sermon notes, each neatly outlined with Roman numerals and capital letters, typed by my mother.

We were not Catholic. We didn't believe in the miracle of transubstantiation. The bread is bread and the juice is juice. It's only a symbol of the body and the blood of Christ. Nothing more. Nothing less. We were not Pentecostal. We didn't believe in speaking in tongues. We didn't slap crippled people on the head and knock them to the ground so that we could watch them stand up and walk again. We didn't handle snakes or writhe on the floor in spiritual ecstasy. We didn't take hallucinogenic drugs so that we could reach out and touch the face of God. No peyote. No Voodoo dolls. No faces of the Virgin Mary in the Three Layer Jell-O. We were pre-tribulation, pre-millennial, fundamentalist Baptists who believed in a literal six-day creation, the Authorized King James Version, Vacation Bible School, the old hymns, potluck dinners, and altar calls at the end of every service. Usually when my father gave an altar call—when he invited those who wished to accept Christ into their hearts, who wished to get right with God, to come forward—no one did. He would stand there alone in front of the altar and wait while we sang yet one more verse of "Just As I Am" or "When I Survey the Wondrous Cross." I always hoped someone would come forward, to give validation to the sermon and to my father, their presence an assurance that all was well. Sometimes I considered going forward myself, just so my father wouldn't have to stand there alone. But I never did. What would the congregation have thought? What reason did I have for going forward? What sins had I committed?

Yet when Rod Rudd gave the altar call at the close of that service, half the congregation streamed forward. Most only wanted to shake his hand or to give him a hug. A few wept. They came right away, came right up, and he smiled at them and greeted them and they bowed right there in prayer while we kept singing, one more verse and then another, the people kept coming, my mother on piano.

I sat in the chair behind my father's desk and spun slowly around. Like the books in the room, the desk was solid, the sort of thing it would take four strong men to move. It spoke to the weightiness of the room, of its purpose. It was here that my father prepared his sermons and Sunday school lessons; it was here that my father rescued failing marriages; it was here that wedding licenses were signed and widowers comforted.

I rose from the swivel chair and stepped around to the front of my father's desk. I put one hand in my pants pocket like Rod Rudd and raised the other to the sky. I stalked the space in front of my father's desk, my hand rising and falling, and I imagined that I was Rod Rudd, that I was a missionary back from the jungles of Africa and that I had amazing stories to tell. I have seen people healed of leprosy with the touch of a hand; I have seen men walk through fire; I have heard animals speak, witnessed the blind made to see, the deaf to hear. I have seen men and women set free from the bondage of sin. I have seen water turned into wine, giants slain by boys with slingshots, and a loaf of bread and five fishes feed five thousand. I was dead, but now I am alive.

We were seated around the dining room table over which my mother had spread her good white tablecloth, the one her grandmother gave to her as a wedding present. Mother had kept things simple. It was just sloppy joes and Jay's potato chips, sweet pickles, carrot sticks, and celery sticks with peanut butter. There would be chocolate cake with ice cream and hot fudge for dessert. My parents sat at each end of the table with Rod Rudd to my father's right and Carolyn Rudd to my mother's left. The Rudd kids sat in-between their parents and we sat opposite them. Well-behaved as always.

Between preachers and missionaries there's a natural empathy, a spirit of shared suffering. The long hours, the low pay, the sense of sacrifice and duty, of being strangers in a strange land. There is the ever-present gaze of the public eye and the sense of living from crisis to crisis. The congregation's needs, your needs; its demands, your responsibilities. Both bear the secrets of their congregations. It isn't all Sunday school and happy songs about Jesus.

It was Rod Rudd who dominated the conversation around the dinner table that night. He told wild stories about Vietnam and Brazil, of bombing runs and the fire and smoke of napalm, of death spirals and pulling G's. There were baptisms in the river and floods and exotic beasts, poison-tipped arrows and cannibal tribes and shallow graves and men with guns. There was death and eternity and military tribunals and the Judgment Seat of Christ. He devoured my mother's sloppy joes with a righteous fervor and complimented my father on the landscaping at the church. When Carolyn told Rod that he should let somebody else talk, he laughed and apologized, admitted it was a vice he had. He liked to tell stories. It was a gift God had given him.

"A gift?" said my mother. "Well, that's one word for it."

Rod laughed. He raised both of his hands before him, palms open to us, like a felon admitting guilt. Then he was off again, ready with another story. "Did you guys know that your mother was once my girlfriend?" he asked us. He had a big, good-natured grin on his face as he slapped my father on the side of the arm. "Can you believe it? And then she went and picked your father over me?! Over me?!"

I looked at my mother, but she had her head down, wiping the sloppy joe mix from her fingers with a paper napkin.

"Let's not talk about that, Rod," Carolyn said. "That's water under the bridge. A long time ago. We were all just kids."

"You were all just kids!" Rod said. He laughed again. He blew Carolyn a kiss. She blushed. My mother asked if she could get anyone anything from the kitchen. No one said, "Yes," but my mother rose any way and disappeared into the kitchen.

Carolyn wore a silk scarf around her neck and a beautiful long peasant dress with a necklace of hand-painted wooden beads and big colorful bracelets. Her long hair, still more blonde than any other shade, was piled high atop her head in a way that seemed carefully effortless. She wore just enough makeup to cover the lines and the wrinkles that had begun to characterize her face, but not enough to attract ridicule or scorn from the ladies in the congregation. Even then I could see why Rod would have preferred Carolyn to my mother. It wasn't that my mother was unattractive—even one of my classmates had once said that my mother was "good looking for a mom," but Carolyn was pretty in a way my mother wasn't, in a way my mother never had been.

Still it didn't mean much to me then, that Rod and my mother had once been boyfriend and girlfriend. I was ten years old and to be boyfriend and girlfriend meant to sit next to each other in church or to hold hands during the couples skate at the roller rink. To exchange valentines or to write your initials and her initials and to connect them with a plus sign.

When my mother returned from the kitchen, she set a plastic two-liter bottle of Coke in the center of the table. "I didn't realize you'd all been through such a time down there," she said. "I mean with the accident and all."

Rod nodded.

"You have no idea," Carolyn said.

"How long was his recovery time? The damage that must have done . . ."

"He was out of the hospital within a day," Rod said. "The doctors couldn't explain it, and when they couldn't explain it, they didn't want anything to do with it. When they found out we were missionaries and when I said it had to be a miracle, they decided to send him home. They called me a witch doctor. Can you believe that? Me? A witch doctor."

Rod laughed, but it was a forced laugh this time, the laugh of some-one who knew that what he said wasn't easy to accept. Even the most faithful understand the unbelief of others.

"But surely they saw the damage the pole had done," my father said.

"There wasn't much to see."

"What do you mean?"

"It was already closing up by the time we reached the hospital. It was healing that fast."

"What about the pole?" my mother asked.

"They couldn't find the pole."

"But it must have been right outside the truck."

"The road was flooded. There was water and mud all over the place. Who knows what happened to it?"

I watched James eat his sloppy joes, his potato chips, drink his pop. I watched him chew, sip, swallow. I watched every turn of his wrist or his neck. I watched him breathe. I wondered how he was different now, how his body had been changed. I wondered if he thought about it every day, if there ever was a moment when he didn't think about it. How he almost died. I wondered if he was thankful, if he gave thanks every morning when he awoke and every night when he lay himself down to sleep. I wondered if he felt like a miracle, like some sort of character from out of the Bible.

"How's the medical services down there, the hospitals?" my father asked.

"Terrible," Carolyn said. "Just terrible."

"Was there much pain?" my mother asked. She was looking at James when she said this but I wasn't sure if she was asking him or Carolyn or Rod.

"It was a metal pole," my father said. He smiled as he said it, like ha-ha, someone drives a pole through your chest of course it's going to hurt.

James looked up at her and nodded. "Yeah, I guess so," he said. "I don't remember much about it. Dad thinks I blacked out."

"Blacked out?" my mother said. "So you don't remember?"

"No, not at all."

"He was lucky that way," Carolyn said.

"I'm sure he was," answered my mother.

There was a skepticism to my mother's voice, a tone I recognized. I began to realize that she didn't fully believe the story, that her questions weren't just dinner table talk, that there was more at stake than I knew. Maybe none of these realizations would form until much later, somewhere down the road as I grew older and learned that the world was not as I had imagined it to be and that faith isn't something that comes easily, if at all. I became aware for the first time of a tension that must have been there from the start, from the moment Rod and Carolyn arrived at the church in their station wagon, the explanation of their tardiness, the futility of assigning blame.

I looked to Rod. He peered across the table at my mother with his head tilted to one side as if anticipating a blow on his left cheek. My mother met his gaze and didn't let it go. She has never been the type to back down, least of all to a man like Rod, the kind of man who assumes she will back down, whose theological convictions say she should back down.

"You should come with us to Brazil," Carolyn said. "If you're so unhappy here."

"Who said we were unhappy?" my mother snapped.

"Well," Carolyn said, but then she stopped.

There was an awkward silence that took over the table and a sense of panic welled up inside me, a panic of being found out, of a secret sin revealed. I wanted to rush in, to fill the silence, to move us beyond this moment, this revelation made bare. Yes, I wanted to confess, she's unhappy. My parents argue every night, after they've sent us to bed, after they think we're asleep. She hollers and screams and threatens to leave my father if he doesn't get her out of this small town; if he doesn't do something to change the way she's treated in this church; if he doesn't do something to improve our financial situation; if he doesn't have the guts to ask for a raise so he can feed and clothe his children. Yes, she's unhappy. But I wondered how Carolyn Rudd knew, wondered who told her of all the unhappiness here.

"I could never live that way," my mother said. "I don't know how you do it."

Rod began to say something about the will of God, but my father interrupted him.

"Why don't you kids go outside and play?" he said. "Run out, burn off some of that energy."

"Play what?" my brother Nathan asked.

"I don't know. A game. Tag."

"What about soccer?" said Rod Rudd. "Our kids love soccer."

"Soccer's a communist sport," I said.

"A what?" my father asked.

"A communist sport," I said. I didn't know what I was talking about. It was just something I'd heard my baseball coach say. "We can play baseball," I said.

"We have a soccer ball in the car," Sara said. And then she was out of her seat and out the door and right behind her went my brothers and my sisters, the traitors. James followed too.

But I stayed. I wanted to hear more stories of miracles. I wanted to listen to Rod Rudd talk about the life of a missionary in Brazil. So I stayed through a second helping of dessert. I stayed through coffee. I crossed my arms in front of me and leaned on the table. But the talk turned to church politics, gossip about old seminary classmates, complaints about aging, recipes for meatloaf. Finally I resigned myself to the tediousness of a summer night in our small town, the day dragging itself toward its conclusion, and excused myself from the table and hurried to find the others.

They had snagged a few kids from the neighborhood—Ryan and Cal and Dustin—and divided into two teams. From the sidelines it appeared chaotic, everyone chasing after the ball, kicking it, and chasing after it again. The local kids didn't know what they were doing. There was no strategy involved, no goal but to get to the ball first and kick it as far as possible in one direction or the other. They hollered to each other—"I'm open! I'm open"—and looked at each other in bewilderment each time Sara called offside. Sara and Luke—both were barefooted on the hard-packed earth field—dominated the game. Sara would sweep the ball onto her foot and head off down the field like a kamikaze pilot, and she and Luke hollered back and forth to each other in Portuguese until Luke became angry and told Sara she was being bossy and that he was joining the other team.

James was nowhere to be seen. When I caught up with Nathan and asked him where James had gone, he pointed toward the playground across the street and down the hill from the elementary school. Then he tore after the ball.

When I found James, he was seated on a wooden step embedded in the hill to the playground, well out of view of the others. He was barefooted with his pant legs rolled halfway up his calves. His tie was wrapped around his head like a bandanna and his shirt was unbuttoned and untucked and he was sweating in the summer heat and humidity. His T-shirt was on the ground beside him.

"Why aren't you playing?" I asked.

I sat myself down beside him.

"None of your business," he said.

He raised his right hand to his lips and I realized that he was smoking a cigarette.

"You smoke," I said.

He tapped the cigarette and a bit of ash fell to the ground between us. "Everybody in Brazil smokes," he said.

"I've never smoked."

"Here," he said. He reached into his pants pocket and pulled out a small foil pack and handed it to me. I hesitated.

"Go on," he said.

So I took the pack and slipped a cigarette into my hand and looked to see how he was holding his. He removed a pack of matches from his pocket and tore off a match and lit my cigarette for me. I put it to my mouth and sucked on the end and then nearly fell over in a fit of coughing. James laughed, but then he too was struck by a fit of coughing. When he stopped, he slipped his hand between the open folds of his shirt and rubbed his bare chest. He winced.

"Does it hurt?" I asked.

"Sometimes."

"Maybe you shouldn't smoke."

"It doesn't hurt because I smoke."

I gave the cigarette back. "Thanks," I said, worried I'd vomit if I tried it again. "That was good."

He laughed.

"Do your parents know?" I asked.

"That I smoke? Are you kidding?"

"No. Do they know that it hurts?"

He shook his head. "No. You're not going to tell them, are you?"

I shook my head.

"Do you want to touch it?" he asked.

I realized I'd been staring at his chest, the scar tissue there, like a large, pinkish mountain range on a relief map. It appeared tender, swollen. I didn't want to touch it. Someone else's body. Someone else's flesh and bone.

"How long has it been?" I asked.

"Almost two years. Go ahead. Touch it."

He turned his body so that his chest was square to me and he pulled back the folds of his shirt. His chest was bony and pale and covered in sweat from playing soccer. I reached out with my hand—it was shaking and I was trying not to act like it was or that I knew that he knew that my hand was shaking. I don't know what I expected I'd feel or what I thought would happen, a bolt of current, like electricity perhaps, or a vibration like an engine or some strange energy field. It's just his chest, I thought. It's just scar tissue.

I placed my hand on the scar, first with just my fingertips and then with the palm. It was smooth to the touch, newborn smooth. I laid my hand flat against his chest and held it there. It couldn't have been for more than a second, I know, but it felt like much longer. In that brief second, I felt the throb of his heart, the muscle expanding and contracting, its rhythm, its pulse. I felt the blood flowing through his body, racing through the arteries and veins, and I felt the sticky dampness of sweat on his skin.

I pulled my hand away. James didn't look at me. We both stared off into the distance, past the trees, to the lake, to the calm surface there.

"Wow," I said.

"No," he said. "No wow."

I entered the house by the back door and I was cutting through the kitchen to the bathroom with the horrible taste of the cigarette in my mouth and the fear that if I didn't lose that taste soon, I would vomit. And then I'd have even more to explain.

"Where are you going?"

It was my mother. There was an edge in her voice and I didn't know where it was coming from. For a moment I thought I'd been caught and I wondered who told on James and me, who it was that saw us smoking and hurried home to tell.

"I just need to pee," I said.

Rod entered the kitchen from the dining room and said, "I'm sorry, Hannah. I truly am." Then he saw me and spun around and walked right back out the way he came in. I looked at my mother and I realized she'd been crying, that her eyes were red and swollen. Carolyn appeared a moment later and asked me where the kids were.

"In the lot next to the school," I said, "playing soccer."

"Could you go get them for me?" she asked.

"Are you leaving?" I asked.

"You heard her," my mother said. "Now go."

I slipped out the kitchen and through the back door. As I started to run down the street toward the school, I saw Rod and my father standing beside the Rudds' station wagon. Rod leaned back against the side panel with his arms crossed. My father shook his head.

We stood in the driveway, all of us, and waved good-bye until Rod Rudd honked the horn and the station wagon disappeared around the corner. Then we went back inside and got ready for bed, then gathered in a cluster in the girls' room upstairs. The girls were stretched across their beds and the boys sat on the floor. My mother sat on Ruth's bed and my father sat on the floor in front of her.

This is how we ended every day in those years, with family devotions. My father began by reading a story about the Muffin twins, Minnie and Max. It didn't take long, maybe three or four minutes. It was a simple children's story with a clear-cut application—do not lie, do not steal, obey your parents, love God. Then we took turns praying. My mother would start and then each of us would say just a line or two, though since I was the oldest I always tried to come up with three or four things to say. That night I only asked God to keep the Rudds safe on their drive home. My father closed, and when he said, "Amen," we all scrambled for our beds.

When my father leaned over to kiss me goodnight—my mother had already gone downstairs and only the hallway night-light remained on— I was thinking about Rod Rudd and fighter planes, about war and landing planes on the Amazon in the midst of a storm. I asked my father why he didn't fight in Vietnam.

"I was in college at the time," he said, "and then I went to seminary, and so I was never chosen in the draft. I had what was called a deferment."

He tried to explain the draft to me, the system of numbers and letters and the lottery, and he mentioned boys from his hometown who died in Vietnam, how sad and confused everyone had been. Then he told me to go to sleep.

Later that night, there was yelling and screaming and crying. My mother sobbed and my father tried to calm her down. A door slammed. I buried my head beneath the blankets, worried that this would be the end, that my mother would leave my father and my father would lose his job and we would all end up homeless. I closed my eyes and prayed to God. I wanted to ask God to drive a metal pole through my heart so that my father could rip it out of me and we could all be saved. But I didn't say this. These were not the kinds of prayers you were supposed to pray, and besides, I kept hearing James saying, "It hurts. It hurts." So instead I closed my eyes tight and prayed that I would fall asleep, fall asleep fast, fall asleep now.

In the morning, I gathered my ball glove and bat and hurried down the stairs, intent on getting out the door before anyone could stop me with a list of chores. But there was no sign of life anywhere in the house and the door to my parents' bedroom remained closed. Outside the car was gone and I remembered that my father had had to drive to Kalamazoo early that morning for Mr. Brubaker's heart surgery.

The morning was bright with sunshine. Already the air promised a day of heat and high humidity. I wore Wrangler blue jeans, a gray T-shirt, and tennis shoes, the white canvas stained from mowing the grass on Saturday morning. I cut across the lot behind the bank and past the used car dealership, then turned up Swan Street. Across the way the elementary school lay dormant in its summer idleness. I wanted to be at the ball diamond by eight to play home run derby. I walked casually, knowing I had plenty of time, that no one else would be there yet and I could take some cuts off the T before the others arrived.

From up the street, a car approached, a blue Ford sedan, the sunlight reflected white off its front windshield. It moved slowly, just below the speed limit, and as it drew closer I imagined myself stepping into its path, the driver trying to swerve at the last moment, but unable to avoid me. I imagined the impact of the grill against my body, my body lifting into the air and tumbling in three different directions at once, then landing hard on the asphalt—on my shoulder, on my the back of my neck, on my head. I heard the grinding of brakes, the squeal of tires, the sirens, voices above me, felt needles poked into my skin. I imagined myself rising from off the asphalt, a boy come back from the dead.

The blue Ford sedan passed, and I walked on, past the dentist's office and past Wanda's Watch Repair. Already I could feel the sweat building on my brow and in the middle of my back. A black dog, a rottweiler, in front of pea-green house rose from its hindquarters and bared its teeth and barked at me. It moved aggressively forward until its chain snapped at the tension. He growled fiercely, strained to move beyond the hard-packed dirt that marked the boundaries of his territory, and I made to move quickly past, lacking confidence in leather collars and steel chains. But then I stopped, drawn to something I heard in his growl, in his bark, a voice, I believed, that was trying to tell me something. So I reversed field and stepped into the yard, the grass uncut for several weeks, patches made bare by dog shit. I walked cautiously forward, bending at the waist, inclining my ear toward the dog. I could smell his breath, see the panting of his thick chest. I tried to make out what he might be saying to me, what wisdom from God he spoke. But there was nothing.

I detoured along the edge of the lake, the path that my parents were always warning me to avoid—street rats and other teenage riffraff hung out there, out of sight of police officers and parents, and they left behind empty beer cans and cigarette butts. When I looked back over my shoulder, I saw the dam and the bridge. I imagined myself stepping out onto the flat surface of the water and walking across it. I imagined raising my baseball bat into the air, like Moses with his rod, the waters of Palmer Lake parting before me. I would walk across on dry land, walk from here to the marina on the other side, right on through town to the IGA.

It would be several years before I would realize that Rod Rudd had been my mother's first lover and everything that that word entailed, and later I would come to realize too that my father had gone to seminary to avoid the war in Vietnam though he would never admit to it as such. But on that morning all those things were beyond my horizon. So I stood on the edge of the lake, its surface calm and nearly white in its reflection of the sun, and collected a handful of stones from the muddy bank. I shook out the small ones and the flat ones until I'd pocketed the set I wanted. I placed the bat on my left shoulder and held it with my left hand, then tossed a stone into the air with my right. I followed the stone to its apex and then, as it fell, I swung away, my hands tight around the narrow handle, my feet unsteady in the moist earth. The first stone trickled into the water and the second I missed completely. It wasn't until the fifth stone— a smooth, pinkish rock—that I caught one square.

There was a crack of the wood against the stone and I followed through with my swing, just as my father had taught me. The stone caught the fat part of the bat and I watched as the stone climbed higher and higher, arching out over the lake. I waited for the stone to fall to earth, to drop into the lake, but instead it only seemed to climb higher, to carry further, and for a moment I found myself holding my breath, wondering what was possible. But then the stone dropped beneath the tree line and I lost sight of it until I saw a small splash of water. I exhaled, let myself breathe. Just a stone. Just gravity. And it was more than I could bear.

CPSIA information can be obtained
at www.ICGtesting.com
Printed in the USA
LVHW090437280221
679762LV00006B/33

9 780814 257319